D1049754

ALSO BY ANN BERK

Fast Forward

LAUGH LINES

Ann Berk

Random House New York

 Published in the United States by Random House, Inc., New York, and simultaneously in Canada by Random House of Canada Limited, Toronto.

Library of Congress Cataloging-in-Publication Data
Berk, Ann.
Laugh lines.
I. Title.
PS3552.E71948L38 1989 813'.54 88-43364
ISBN 0-394-55644-5

Book design by Debbie Glasserman

Manufactured in the United States of America
24689753
First Edition

For my mother and father

"She was a faded but still lovely woman of twenty-seven."

—F. SCOTT FITZGERALD, *Early Success*

I wish to thank Kate Medina and Robert Gottlieb for their unstinting support, Barbara Haynes for reading and listening, my daughter, Melinda, for her love and unshakable confidence, and my husband, Louis Romano, for absolutely everything.

LAUGH LINES

one

t 3:00 A.M. Georgie sat on the bare tiles in her nightgown, poised over the toilet bowl in earnest prayer. Nothing was coming up, nothing would, leaving her to wish she could take off her head like a hat.

She remembered diving into the kitchen as if propelled by a wind, thighs forward, arms outstretched . . . something about a dinner party, the greasy aftermath, Saran Wrap entangled around her arms ensuring freshness . . . a soft bounce into the double-door, frost-free, ice-making refrigerator, floating off light as a feather, carried by the wind.

Later she had lain in the bed on her side of it, in her own groove, like a stone. She heard the sound of her labored breathing and tried to concentrate, struggling at each intake of air, each wheezing exhalation, overcome with chills, her lips dry, her tongue dry, the roof of her mouth like dry paste. She was stunned by her drunkenness, if that's what it was; it could be death. More likely it was cream sherry. She knew you didn't have to drink it in those silly little glasses. She'd poured it into a water goblet with her pinkie extended, a stab at daintiness in the face of intemperance. Her cheeks burned. The sherry was sweet, syrupy, vaguely reminiscent of cough medicines that had made her gag as a child. She'd poured and poured, with the reckless abandon of a wife whose dinner guests had continued hurling culinary praise at her lingering shadow all the way to their cars.

This pre-Christmas dinner, a ritual for which she had acquired a measure of local fame, had been put together completely that very day. Georgie was not one to prepare in advance; she found such women bloodless, suspect. How much more daring to place oneself at the edge, what indisputable proof of one's value to pull it off! It was true that the decorations had been hung in advance, the tree trimmed, the house polished for inspection. But the house was always polished, a reflection of Georgie's frustration at not having a proper career, of the dearth of orgasmic thrills in her marital bed, or of her need to exercise meticulous control over surrounding surfaces ever since her body had begun running wildly to fat, depending upon which psychiatrist she was paying at the time.

At 4:00 A.M. she tried to work the convenient, considerate reading light Lew had given her, but her fingers attacked the clip-on contraption with the dexterity of a toddler. Her heart was pounding; she needed the light. She switched on the night-table lamp and turned to watch the back of Lew's head for a sign, but he didn't stir. In a rush of tenderness she reached to pull the sheet up, making an awning over his eyes; it fell flat on his face.

At 5:30 Lew still hadn't moved. And Georgie, having

lurched into the bathroom, twice now, like a blimp with an air hole, could stretch her legs deep into the bed and feel some small comfort. She was grateful that if the night had eyes, they belonged to strangers; she disgusted herself. Where was the girl who could drink whatever she wanted and never become sloppy, hair hanging, face sagging, a faintly putrid odor in her wake—where was she? Right, old girl, Georgie said to herself, mourn your youth for its tolerance for alcohol, that's the thing we miss as the years trundle by, that's the nub of it.

She tried forgiving herself. After all, her day had started at 6:00 A.M., Georgie alone in her kitchen, raw elements laid out, every conceivable tool in place for this gourmet operation. And she had worked hard, cooking up a storm, a veritable culinary crescendo, mopping up the spoils along the way. By four in the afternoon she was snug in the tub, perhaps a bit snugger than she would have liked owing to her girth. But there was no time to loll around, floating thoughts; the guests, good neighbors, were all there by six.

Georgie had come to greet them in an orange caftan trimmed in gold, which allowed for bigness, lushness, but hid the specificity of fat. Her delicately arched feet were visible in gold sandals; her gold earrings dangled, tinkled, gleamed. Lew stood beside her in a three-piece blue suit with a wild dash of red poking from his breast pocket, leaning toward the door as if preparing to pull people in. He made offerings from a huge crystal bowl brimming with the eggnog that he had prepared, a long-standing ritual Georgie deeply appreciated, as the stuff reminded her of Kaopectate. And so the evening began.

She outdid herself every year, of course. This time she had set out roast duck with sausage-and-apple stuffing, braised onions, *crêpes de pommes de terre,* brussels sprouts, wine and hard cider, cold soufflés, hot traditional pies. Mavis helped, as always, sliding things in and out of the oven or the refrigerator according to Georgie's precisely written instructions, tromping into the living room, her shoulders stiff with contempt, when it was time for Georgie to garnish the platters, something which she, Mavis, could well have done herself.

Georgie and Lew's children, two in college and one working at her first job, were all home for Christmas and had even made an appearance during cocktails. They had shone with adulthood, startling their parents' friends, who had known them all their lives; it was the shock of recognition, one's own mortality in the eyes of other people's children. Georgie herself had been thinking, as she dressed, of the girl she had been; of putting on makeup to the sounds of Sinatra or The Four Freshman, slipping into a little black dress, butterflies in her stomach, a quivering heart. Instead, here was Georgie gliding through the room to touch her husband, a public gesture performed by rote, designed to declare solidity to people with problems of their own. She raised her cigarette holder expectantly, as if it was a wand that could work its magic and wave it all away; all of this grown-up business, this marriage, this house, this dinner party, her life.

She had been shaken from her usual state, a dull despair as manageable and oddly comforting as any small infirmity, by a conversation in her kitchen that afternoon. The phone had rung and rung and Georgie, furiously busy, had picked it up to stop it. "Yes," she'd snapped, not even "hello." When she'd recognized Beth's voice she was immediately sorry to have greeted her old friend with anything other than warmth; even sorrier to have exposed her nerves in her one successful arena, the kitchen.

Beth's news, the possibility that she was pregnant, again, took repeating before it sank in, closing Georgie's mouth like a clamp. She stared at the wallpaper until its small pattern blurred her vision. Knee-deep in duck dressing and fluffy egg whites in her Larchmont kitchen, she felt herself float to some other place and come back some other person. Georgina she had been then, Georgina Brand. She was at Carlisle University, living with Beth and the third link in their tight circle, Suzanne, dreaming of this very life; no, surely not this one; the thought snapped her out of her trance. But what were they doing talking about the fear of pregnancy *now,* in their mid- to late forties? Had Beth gone mad? They were tasteful ladies, who wore one-piece bathing suits, chewed calcium and knew sex wasn't all it was cracked up to be. Or was that just the married ones? Beth and Suzanne were divorced, single again: inhabitants of that other place where no one was allowed to get old and sex was better than they'd dreamed.

And so Georgie had promised Beth that she'd arrange for their threesome to come together imminently, as was their pattern when any one of them was in need. Then she tucked herself in, stuffed the ducks and licked her fingers, all the while singing "The Man Who Never Returned" for the very first time since her college days. She remembered every word.

Tapping her fingers on the headboard, she counted the years since graduation—twenty-five in all. She had wanted to hurry up time in those days. Now, when she wanted only to linger, having nowhere to run, nowhere in particular to go, she felt as if she was getting her period every other week; as if chunks of her life were unaccountably gone before she had even gotten to touch them. How was she to navigate when she couldn't get her bearings? When she couldn't even fathom how she'd let herself become so fat that she was shocked by her own mirror image day after day? This made her keep a tight rein on herself, as she had tonight, if only for the illusion of control.

Yet she took pride in her ability to keep the secrets of her life from her companions in it; other women might be spillers, weepers, whiners, but not Georgie. Only her old roommates knew the real truth of her, or some of it. She had no intention of moving about in the world unarmed.

Was that what all this fat was—armor? Camouflage? Clever Georgie, hiding the tight, desperate coil that was herself beneath jolly, jiggling folds.

Thus, at her dinner party, she had not evidenced the smallest clue that her senses, so carefully disciplined for general view, were in fact charged and crackling. It was Beth's news, Beth's story, having no direct effect on Georgie's life. But it had hurtled her back to that clean, generous place, her girlhood, where she had worn her young heart like a new dress and believed passionately in love.

She wondered what Beth and Suzanne had been thinking all these years, watching her grow beyond reason, watching Lew prosper. Was there envy, ever, for the soundness of her husband and home, as they made their way singly through unpredictable tides, imagining her so safely anchored? But surely they knew better. Appalled at her relentless girth but wisely keeping their explications more or less to themselves, they let her emote from her wifely throne, saving her place.

Did she envy *them*? They both had formidable careers, romance, their own co-ops; they didn't parallel park. But Suzanne was in love with a married man. Or more precisely, Georgie thought, she was in love with the emotion-charged pulse of it, playing the heroine when in fact she'd taken the victim's part. And Beth, all beauty and grace, seemed to move like a sleepwalker from man to man, placing herself in temporary service, her will suspended, her intellect on hold.

Still, Georgie *did* envy them. She envied them their possibilities, if only because they still strained after them. Her own desires had dried up, her hopes had become old memories.

Georgie wondered if it was all a matter of timing—had they each been set on their respective paths by a moment here, an instant there? Here was Beth, under threat of pregnancy yet again, the circumstances tenuous again—for Georgie had just seen Beth's lover, Robert, with an extremely young woman, a girl really, her hair permed to surprise as if she, too, wondered at his rapt attention. They had merely been walking, not even touching, but as Georgie watched him speak, as she watched his slow smile and the girl's wide-eyed gaze, she knew he was making a conquest, and an easy one at that. She made certain Robert saw her; made certain he knew she saw *him.* Hoping to give him pause, and the sleepless nights of the culpable who might be found out.

In the morning the winter sun rolled across Georgie's eyes like hot butter. Her head pounded. She turned to look at Lew and had her first sober thought—why, she was just like Beth; she, too, had disavowed her past, set part of her life aside as if it had never happened. But she had failed miserably, suffocating all sense of feeling, of caring, when she had only meant to take cover.

Doomed to excess.

two

Beth was that seemingly perfect combination in a world that allowed its women out of the kitchen: beautiful and smart. Of course, intelligence does not pack the instant wallop of an eyeful. And so it was the long and lustrous hair, the rare bluish eyes that were nearly gray, the full, lush breasts, the hard body promising softness that caused men to suck in their breaths. She had always been grateful for her looks, yet there were times when she longed for an ethereal aura, a subtle presence. Instead she generated fire, like a bodice-busting temptress out of pulp fiction.

Women, too, had always watched her, their narrowed eyes taking in this nearly perfect model of their gender as they shrank within themselves. Beth had always known this and was not discomfited anymore; now that she was older, they were more forgiving. Thus she could roam the aisles of this female haven, a department store, seeking relief, and perhaps even finding it.

She watched them as they examined gloves, belts and scarves with that great sense of purpose women seem to have when they give themselves over to the art of choosing, deciphering. She watched them perched on stools, shopping bags at their feet, leaning hopefully toward the wispy young men at cosmetic counters who would redesign their faces, their lives. She knew what serious business transpired in stores such as this, where one could be temporarily delivered from misery and dread as well as from the rain or the cold.

Beth suddenly trembled from a wave of nausea, and held on to a counter to steady herself. She had not yet told Robert, the man with whom she lived, that he was in danger of responsibility: that she might be pregnant. But then pregnancy seemed hardly possible at her age, even somehow repugnant—a thought that shocked her the moment she had it. What on earth did she mean, that sex was repugnant at her age? This was rot, she knew it; she also knew that as her body's slow, natural aging process had lately accelerated, her vision had begun to shift. So had her perception of propriety. The fact that her looks had quite literally stopped traffic had afforded her a sense of purity: she'd had nothing whatever to do with her own beauty, after all; she'd just borne it with acceptance. But now, when quiet appreciation followed in her wake rather than the startled eyes that had once beheld her, she was suddenly very conscious of her looks, and of her desire to hold on to them. Conscious of aging altogether; fearful of its ramifications. Yet she hadn't made a profession of her beauty—she was a woman of no small accomplishment, a columnist carried in hundreds of newspapers. Then why was she filled with a physical dread, why did it feel embarrassing, even unseemly, to contemplate pregnancy at the age of forty-six? All right, forty-seven next month.

She had considered using one of those do-it-yourself pregnancy test kits, but to someone of her generation it sounded about as reliable as "I promise I won't come inside you." She would wait to see her gynecologist, the only man she knew who could satisfy her with the word no: no, that's not a lump, it's a fibroid cyst; no, you're not pregnant, just experiencing a little hormonal havoc. She longed for a heightened perspective on the body's inevitable nasty tricks.

The nausea, she knew, meant nothing; that is, it didn't necessarily mean that she was pregnant. It could mean that she was coming down with the flu, or that she was scared, apprehensive. In high school she'd thrown up before her French final; nausea and anxiety were old friends. Even a missed period or two was common enough at her age, and generally the forerunner of an entirely different altered state.

Still, she knew the law of averages might finally have caught up with her. Part of her had already succumbed to the possibility of a child; there were moments when she felt as if she had stumbled into a cave where the air especially suited her, where motherhood was simply another outfit to slip into and wear with natural ease. Until she got dizzy from the wishful rethinking of her life.

A woman in a raccoon coat and red scarf was having her face made up. Even with her eyes closed she flinched under the cruel beam of the fluorescent lamp aimed at her imperfections. Watching her, noting the peach fuzz, the flakiness, the creases on her face being subjected to the unforgiving light, Beth felt the woman's vulnerability as her own, as if they were joined. Yet they would probably be of no help to each other. Unlike men, who had perfected nonchalance by their years of exposure standing side-by-side at urinals, most women couldn't stop looking at their own kind, measuring, taking inventory whenever they got the chance. Beth reached for a sample of moisturizer, certain her thirsty skin would drink it in.

She would have said she was not there to buy things, not one to be soothed by a purchase. Yet she soon found herself in a dressing room armed with a mound of blouses, skirts and dresses to try on. It was as if she thought she could find rejuvenation, even renewal, if she draped herself in just the right garment, held her head at just the right jaunty angle and headed back out into the world at just the right graceful pace, in, of course, the right shoes. She stood for a moment looking at herself in the triple mirror, seeing sides and angles she only saw when she was in such rooms. She felt enveloped, surrounded by this strange image of herself, a woman she didn't altogether recognize, who seemed to have lost her equilibrium. She tried on everything at hand, looking for the right cover to fix the image, to set it right.

Robert was away skiing. Beth did not like to ski, mostly because she hated the cold. That hadn't stopped her from going with him in the past, and happily. But this time she had a column overdue and her mind had been flat, barren; weren't her columns always overdue, wasn't her mind racing? But she had felt Robert's hesitation, a heartbeat of silence where once there had been unbridled enthusiasm. She was an old hand at endings; she knew when a man was beginning to pull away. And so she had begged off the ski trip, averting confrontation when she needed all of her strength for the more immediate problem at hand.

She heard an anxious voice from the dressing room next door. "Did I tell you I saw them? Let's be mature about this, he says, a fifty-two-year-old man with his arm around a girl who is three years older than our daughter, let's be grown-ups. So I look at her size-four body and refrain from smashing it with my size-twelve hulk. I even keep the steak knife in my pocketbook instead of cutting out his heart, or cutting off his—I'm shushing, I'm shushing!" There was the clanking of jewelry, and the harsh, discordant sound of forced laughter meant to disguise pain. Beth was at once empathetic toward this wife who'd been exchanged for a younger model, and alert to the possibility for a column, which her mind seized upon. Age! All the years one never thinks about it, simply taking for granted that whatever happens there is always time, time to get over it, to make it right, to start again. Until suddenly you smash into a stone wall and that's it; no more time. It feels as if it happened overnight, as if there was an arbitrary line and suddenly, without knowing it, you crossed it. You look in the mirror and search for yourself. Who are you now? Where is your place in the world? For as your face and body alter, your status changes. You are received, perceived, valued differently; perhaps even discarded. Unless, of course, you're a man.

But Beth was losing her train of thought, examining her neck. She had looked in the mirror at that once-graceful connection, and was shocked by the new, crepey skin that had grown there. She wondered if she could ever have thought, with the fatuousness of youth, that the delicate porcelain surface of her skin was hers to keep, that it would never crack. But she must have, for here she was, mesmerized by the pattern of crisscrosses that had tracked across her throat—overnight, surely. She pulled her turtleneck sweater on hastily, and resolved to finish the column when she got home.

Of course, she knew that few things are as they seem. The woman in the dressing room next door might be a harridan, a witch; the girlfriend could be brilliant, a peace corps volunteer, a teacher of autistic children! Then again, she was probably just young. Beth remembered what young was like; that young was always certain and often unwise. She herself, a certifiable fifties girl who reached womanhood in the early sixties, had not been a virgin when she married. Ah, but she was supposed to be; that was the difference. Nothing had turned out as planned, but then their plans had been so limited. She had gotten married, did not have the expected children, and got the unexpected divorce. And somewhere in those years she had taken a turn onto the path that led to her life's work as a writer: greatest surprise of all.

No. The greatest surprise of all was that even with a profession that surpassed any of her girlhood dreams, she still cared so awfully about how she looked.

She bought a blue silk shirt because she thought it gave her a cool, unruffled façade—hoping to mask the lack of control she felt within. She handed her charge card to the saleswoman, who recognized her name: "Just like the writer. It *is* you, isn't it? I read you all the time but my daughter's the one, always quoting you, like the one you just did for Christmas, 'giving is relieving,' right? Wait till I tell her I met you and you're even prettier than your picture; some of those columnists use the same picture for twenty years. Well. Enjoy." Beth saw the woman's sudden shyness at having gone on too long with no response, but she hadn't anything in her today for strangers.

The nausea returned as she searched for a taxi. She told herself she probably wasn't pregnant and what had she imagined in any event, that this would be the baby she'd keep? The truth was, this was the one she wouldn't even have. She was a single woman in mid-life who didn't have a man so much as she had various men, albeit one at a time, at one- or two- or even three-year stretches. Could she go home to this one, to Robert, and say, guess what, you lucky fellow? Worse, she didn't know what she could possibly say to *herself*; she'd been pregnant before, had not been ready back then, and she was past being ready now. All those years ago, when she was pregnant, she had made a wrenching decision out of sheer panic, a kind of hysteria peculiar to those who had passed through adolescence in the fifties and knew exactly what a "bad girl" was. Now she was a woman in the process of shedding her skin, the luminosity of youthfulness and hopefulness. She would become someone else entirely, some other being, forced to move about exposed as never before, vulnerable with age. And so she was thinking about the second half of her life; about endings, not beginnings.

When the bleeding started she was lying on her bed in her coat and boots. She lived in an old apartment building with a heating system often described as suffocating, but Beth considered it perfect. She didn't say this to Robert. She didn't say, I'd rather not go skiing because I hate the cold, the wind will get inside me and ice my bones and I will feel alone with this question I am carrying, this fear of pregnancy come to haunt me again. Instead, she said I have work to do, deadlines to meet; he knew better. He said, I'll stay if you'd rather, and she *would* rather, but she told him to go, he'd been working so hard and it wasn't as if there were children around who would toddle out on Christmas morning full of expectations. He'd be home for New Year's after all, when it counted.

She didn't say *I'm not going because you don't really want me to go.* She didn't say much that was true lately.

The phone rang three times before Beth was certain she had heard it.

It was Georgie. "Did I wake you?" she asked. Then, "I've arranged for our lunch, as promised. Saturday's good for Suzanne—is it all right with you?"

And Beth roused herself to say yes, yes of course it was all right. The lunch was for her, after all. She was the one who had called for help, and she couldn't bring herself to say the crisis has passed; she wasn't sure it had.

Then she lay back, her woman's flow filling her with sorrow and relief.

three

When Georgie called asking that the three of them meet, Suzanne knew that something was up; something always was. Since their college days they had brought one another their seismic moments like offerings, on chipped plates or shiny platters, that might finally satisfy the gods.

Over the years there had been various marital and career crises, Georgie's ovarian cyst, the bee sting that had caused such a horrific reaction in Suzanne's daughter, Annie, that they thought they might lose her, this miscarriage, that injustice. There had been the death of Beth's father; a hysterectomy rightfully diverted; having to put a pet to sleep; the shock of gray hairs; an office affair: fear, loss, depression, anxiety, need. It wasn't that they didn't share any of this with those who were part of their everyday lives, but within this circle, where their adult dreams had begun, they could peel off their everyday faces and take up their histories wherever they had left off, in the finely honed shorthand of their private knowledge. And if they didn't tell one another everything, for of course they didn't, their books on one another had only occasional misjudgments; even then, rewrites and revisions were often the cause. Effortlessly, instinctively, they'd created a crisis center that eschewed anonymity, preferring the magnified view intimacy afforded; counting on it. And when it was one of the other two who signaled for help, this allowed for the illusion, however momentary, that one's own life was carefree.

Suzanne, for example, an art director and senior vice president at an advertising agency, had spent the morning working on a major campaign for a new yogurt that had only 150 calories and tasted like chalk, glowing all the while with the memory of her lover's adoration the night before. Dale, the copywriter working on the yogurt account with her, and an old friend, had only to glance at Suzanne to recognize the source of her sheen, which would, he knew, be gone in a relative flash, just as her lover had gone, as usual, back home to his wife.

Suzanne and Dale had been a team for several years at Damon & Moore, once the quintessential hard-sell agency that created commercials in which unattractive characters yelled irksome phrases that passed for selling points. Now they were the purveyors of thirty-second expositions reflecting the real meaning of American life as imagined by people who lived in New York; partners in crime.

And how they'd suffered together, squeezing out campaigns, the dryness within them sometimes interminable until one or the other would suddenly find enough juice to pull them through. One of them always did. At those times they felt the burn of shame at what they did for a living, an embarrassment that they learned early on they shared. For, inevitably, those were the times when they relied on the agility they'd acquired over many professional years to please a client whose product seemed absolutely devoid of meaning or worth. Vaginal deodorant was their favorite of the genre: Sultry Sable, Autumn Fire, Herbal Heat . . . Oh BAsil, BAby!

There were good days, of course, even the possibility of creating that peculiar modern art form, media magic, for an insatiable, barely discerning audience. But Suzanne was unable to consider this talent as anything more than a shiny glibness: whimsy, humor, drama or apple pie, served up by a deft short-order cook who longed instead to go the distance, to create something of *real* value, by which Dale told her she would always mean something beyond her ability.

As she waited for him to put the finishing touches on the copy, Suzanne sketched a variety of female characters for the spot, as types they would choose between for the final storyboard. Women; of course women—who else could be lured so easily by the promise of flat bellies and toned thighs? They wouldn't exactly come out and say it, but they'd show it: a girl of twenty perhaps, miraculously jiggle-free as she runs or jumps or dances, the flawless picture of health, having never had lower-back pain, polyps, dry skin, children. As she worked, Suzanne assured herself that no one of her entire acquaintance would for a moment swallow the implied connection between the yogurt and the nymphet, disremembering that she herself had swallowed the yogurt on several occasions when an edible dinner would have been the norm, and had felt virtuous and thin. What was it about females and food? Preparing it was still a badge of womanhood, yet eating it required some sort of delicate overlay; the fat lady's small, steady bites.

She remembered a Christmas Eve from the past when, freshly married, she and her best friends had come together proudly with their husbands—herself with Mark, Beth with Donald, Georgie with Lew—and shared a woefully undercooked turkey at Beth's apartment, noticing only the wine, the ambiance, the adultness of it all. Of course, later, food became more serious, nutrition for the children, culinary art for one's friends. And later still, denial became proof of self-love. How many lifetimes had passed? They'd shed their husbands—all but Georgie, who was still just barely married to Lew. Beth's column was read in newspapers across the country, the commercials Suzanne helped create were viewed by millions, and Georgie, who had been what they'd all assumed they would be, wife to husband and house, full-time mother to her kids, was twice the size of her natural self.

It seemed to Suzanne that it would be especially unkind for Beth to find herself pregnant now. Her only other pregnancy had occurred when she was a single girl in college, and borne a tragedy that was no less painful for its commonness. Suzanne had often wondered what it was like for Beth to live out her life without children, having given up the one child she had had out of a terrible fear that emanated, one could see now with horror, from a fifties sense of seemliness, a recognition of the necessity of the illusion, if not the reality, of one's virginity. They'd all have done the same thing, probably, for they had reached womanhood during the decade that deified what each successive decade systematically peeled away and shrilly derided. And here was Beth, threatened by a female snare again. In those days, pregnancy had the whiff of melodrama; now it reeked indelicately of farce.

Suzanne had been absently sketching a pregnant woman

when Dale cautioned her that this particular yogurt might prove to be laced with nitrites; ever conscientious, he had tasted it too. They spent the remainder of the morning polishing the storyboard that would be offered, along with two others already completed, to the client that afternoon. Then they met with the account executive and formulated their strategy.

Later, as she made the presentation in a conference room jammed with people from the client side, all of whom were intent on making a contribution to the meeting if only to justify their presence, Suzanne was at the top of her form. After reading animatedly through the first two boards, each projecting a slightly different copy approach, she paused for questions and reactions, banking on the third board—which held the campaign she would recommend—to answer their objections, assuage their hesitations, fulfill their unwittingly stated desires. Dale and the account executive listened respectfully, innocently, as she maneuvered the reactions around the room by restating them, as if for verification, when in fact she was subtly rewording them, building support for the campaign not yet presented. When she finally launched into it there was a bewildering silence, a fraction of a moment when Dale and the account man and Suzanne herself thought they'd lost it, their hearts frozen in their throats; then the applause broke out, beginning with the company president, whose hands came together in a sharp slapping sound, followed by lesser though equally enthusiastic hands all around the room.

Elated, they phoned in the good news to the agency and stopped at a café to celebrate, finding its overdone decorations and Christmas-oriented Muzak not only forgivable but delightful. After two serious drinks the account executive, a happy man, left to make his way to Grand Central and Chappaqua.

Dale and Suzanne nursed their wine and grinned sheepishly; had they failed it would have seemed monumental, yet success loomed from another orbit entirely, a place where one got away, quite easily, with murder.

Dale ordered a plate of hors d'oeuvres, knowing she wanted to linger, the work day having succumbed to the vicissitudes of night. Her children had already gone out West to spend Christmas with their father, and of course she missed them, but it was Neal whose absence hung there, like a mobile without wind. What did other lovers of married men do, how did they survive the American ritual of Christmas, with its insistence on proper families, proper cheer, the men stepping back into their spot by the fire as if hitting a theatrical mark, ennobled by Norman Rockwell, sanctified by Currier & Ives? She would see Neal less and less as the holidays drew nearer, suffering the strain of all that joy alone. It already showed.

Dale regaled her with gossip and she listened, thinking she was insulated by another life entirely, sealed into an intensely private island of inordinately refined, shimmering sand on which she waited, on tiptoe, leaving no footprint, no trace. Only she and Neal knew the waters surrounding them, and how to traverse them. Or it was Neal who knew, and she who somehow adapted, seemingly effortlessly, to his zigzag gait. He thought it miraculous she could do this, and attributed it to her uniqueness and her innate sense of him. But she did not feel unique, nor was she certain at times that her antennae weren't hooked up to Oz.

It was not that she was unaware of the common, pathetic ring to her situation, its basic cheesiness and predictability. It was not that she knew no fear. When Neal announced, at the last possible moment before he left her the evening before, that he and his wife were going away for Christmas, her face had paled, crumbled. "Going away" was so laden with imagined or exaggerated meaning—the intimacy of travel, the very idea of their making plans together. He had said, "Don't worry," as he always said at such curves in their coupling, and she had willed her mouth to close, to soften. For he had talked, all during dinner, about their future, their marriage. And he had come bearing presents for her children, Daniel and Annie, and a small, beautifully wrapped package for her which he pressed her to open right then, a delicate gold necklace which she was never to take off, a card that spoke of "more love than I ever dreamed possible."

It was not that she didn't see her life measured in inches as she held out for this celluloid version of true romance. But she could not seem to help it; it was as if she had been pricked with an adolescent poison that coursed through her system and would not be purged. This was her second "Christmas" with Neal.

"Listen," Dale commanded. In deference to the dinner crowd now snaking its way in, the Muzak holiday hit parade had been replaced by Ella Fitzgerald. They settled back, enveloped by the comfort of this sound they understood, the rhythm of their dreams. Dale looked at his old friend, at Suzanne's fair, nearly luminous skin and brown hair, her symmetrical, rather ordinary features that would not add up to a look of any particular distinction had it not been for her brows, thick and straight and seemingly protective of her hazel eyes. He understood that Suzanne felt love as a reprieve, as if Neal held the key to her worth. Yet by its very nature such a coupling as theirs permitted only a scratching of the surface, the headiness of protracted beginnings. And to Dale, her worth so clearly transcended this tired affair, its worn path to nowhere, that he could not imagine what possessed her. He supposed he had never really understood women; a man waited for him at home, a fact of his life that Suzanne had accepted as readily as someone else might have countenanced the color of his hair. He loved her for it.

"You were tremendous today," Dale said, looking her straight in the eye.

She smiled. "Do you remember Martin, the stockbroker? I don't know what brought him to mind."

"Longley's suit, shirt, shoes, Rolex, perhaps his ultimate driving machine?" Dale said, referring to the president of the yogurt company, remembering Martin precisely.

"Aha. I was just thinking how hard I tried to be desirable to him; no, acceptable, that was it. And all I got was this look of polite horror. Well, it was shortly after the divorce, the kids were in that attitude of looking at every man who came around like he was spoiled meat. And I was so frantic, I wanted to take them, the dog, my stretch marks—all the baggage that came with me—and lock it in a room somewhere as if it never existed; I wanted lightness and gentility and the heat of expectation; I wanted my body back, my youth!"

"And now?"

She seemed surprised by the question. After all, now she was loved.

"Another day like today wouldn't be bad."

four

Georgie drove into town for her lunch with Beth and Suzanne, unwilling to hoist her girth onto a commuter train. She was more and more aware of her obesity lately, especially whenever she stepped beyond the bounds of Larchmont.

It was peculiar how a town, even a neighborhood, could surround one with a wall of safety, built by mere familiarity. In Edgemore Terrace they knew Doug Wren's wife went a bit far with other men, but never too far, and only when she'd had too many stingers; they knew the Blandford's Mercedes and paintings and pied-à-terre came from her money, not his, but he enjoyed these things so well that it gave his wife pleasure; they knew Georgina Gregory was overweight and perhaps even overdone, but she was a magnificent cook and hostess, a woman who did what the other women did yet gave it a spin, that little extra something they could all bask in rather than envy, for she so generously spilled over with life. Georgie knew what they knew and was grateful. Manhattan was another place altogether, where people were as likely to look with merciless eyes as bother to look at all.

She liked the tunnel, always chose that route. An impatient driver everywhere but there, she approached it as her children did their presents when they were young, longing to know what awaited them yet happy to remain in the dark, in that wondrous state of anticipation. The winter sunlight was blindingly painful as she emerged, reminding Georgie that she was a grown-up.

She'd given herself time to park, it being absolutely necessary that she find a lot close by, within a matter of steps. Blast the Russian Tea Room, sitting in the middle of nowhere! Still, she'd arranged for them to have the front banquette, swoosh, she'd be snug in her seat, animated, holding court, from the table top up merely an earthy, buxom woman with a rather glowing face. And so she was.

Beth, on the other hand, was late, her entrance nearly wasted, beauty queen on a short runway, causing only a medium stir. She looked tired.

"You look tired," Georgie said.

Beth hugged her anyway, then embraced Suzanne. She was startled at the different feel of their frames, especially the nearly skeletal quality of Suzanne's. She held her back to look at her, and welcomed the softness of Suzanne's face as if it were a barometer of health.

They ordered their usual, Beth's Scotch with a twist for medicinal warmth, Georgie's red wine, which, she believed, had too few calories to count, and Suzanne's Lillet, a habit acquired in a family of Frenchmen.

"We always say," Beth said, "that we ought to do this more often, not just when there's a *cri de coeur.*"

"Ah, but *chèrie,* as the Frenchman said to his eager mistress, if we did it more often, it would lose its . . . *je ne sais quoi,*" Georgie said, not affecting Suzanne in the least since "mistress" was not a term she applied to herself.

They laughed with the abandon of old friends who still see the child in the mature face before them and are privy to nearly every penetrating, crafty, joyous, raging thing stamped upon it. They were as attuned to one another as when they were girls, brought together by the whim of a college administrator: Beth, the government child from Maryland, whose family home was graced by an ever-present American flag, showy cloak of honor; Georgie, from Illinois, already straining at the leash of her wealthy, insulated Midwestern enclave, hungry for real life; and Suzanne, from New York City, whose parents had fled France in the wake of the Anschluss and produced American children. All through college they'd shared their hopes and their clothes in a variety of dormitory rooms, the smell of Suzanne's paints, the peck of Beth's typewriter and Georgie's flamboyance filling each new space easily, comfortably.

They grew intensely close; there was no place to hide nor would they have wished it, not then. They boasted of harboring no secrets; mystery had still to be learned or craved. They could not yet imagine their separate lives, even as every waking thought and every daydream and every boy they would have died for propelled their speculation. They would be friends forever, having experienced an extraordinary intimacy for the first, and, they vaguely sensed, the last time in their lives.

They chattered now about their men as they always had except during their girlhoods, when they were certain that soon they'd gain entry into the Land of Happy Endings, that amorphous bubble tied with ribbons by Disney bluebirds. Suzanne allowed that Neal would be away for the holidays, while Beth saw the creases around her eyes, the line newly formed above her lip, and wondered how much time Suzanne thought she had left for these games of love and deception, how soon she might sink into that hard thinness of New York women of indeterminate age, whose only desire is maintenance. Or was Beth thinking of herself? It was always a shock, at each turning of one's life, to have become "them": the grown-ups, the parents, the Republicans, the older women.

Then it was Beth's turn. She explained that Robert, whom she lived with, was off skiing alone (or more precisely, without Beth) as she was too far behind in her work, while Georgie thought: Could the rat be with that little girl I saw him with, which, one could argue, was no different from being alone? Would he dare? Must I trade in this currency of women, telling what I don't really know so as to offer faithful protection, running the risk of triggering what has not yet occurred? And why am I always the one left to her own devices? Find your own way out of that dreary play, your life, Georgie; we have big scenes to rehearse!

Beth and Suzanne then inquired about Lew, and Georgie said he was fine, everything was fine, the general lie of her life, which no longer drew comment from these two old hands, her best friends. She had to admit she was thankful.

Their drinks arrived, and Beth proffered a toast. "To false alarms," she said, to the clinking of their glasses and their punctuations of relief, followed by gentle admonishments for holding back the good news.

"I didn't tell you right away because I wanted to see you and

I guess I thought everyone was too busy . . . well, the holidays and all. Maybe I just liked the idea of being in the center of the circled wagons."

It was, they knew, a reliving of the past that had caused Beth to feel so vulnerable, for by comparison this latest problem would have been handled with, if not dispatch, at least a clear eye, pregnancy now being outside the realm of nightmare. And with an intuitive sense it had taken years to refine, gliding among them now so easily, they recognized the panic hovering over Beth, and believed it to emanate from a wound long healed over, now rubbed raw. It was one thing to give up a child for adoption when you were hardly more than a child yourself; quite another to be "unsuitably" pregnant again in your forties—your second chance having turned up as most probably your last.

"She's twenty-five," Beth said, referring to the baby she had carried during her college days, through the summer months and half of her senior year. "Did you know that? I hadn't thought of it before, I never marked off milestones on some calendar in my head—you know, when she would be walking, talking, driving. But these last few weeks, when I thought I might be pregnant again, it was as if the specter of that child was standing over me, watching to see what I would do this time. I became conscious of her and so I had to acknowledge that she exists. And I was angry with her, with the memory—after all, wasn't it fair that I be left alone to live my life as if none of this had happened, as I've always done?"

"Stop beating on yourself," Suzanne said, touching her hand.

Beth's face was suddenly flushed. "But that's just the point—I never have."

"Ah, guilty of not feeling guilty enough," Georgie said. "Obviously you should have been struck dumb, rendered immobile, at the very least made to wear a bra in 1971."

"I like that last one—very uplifting," Beth said.

"Expiating your sins always is. So I've heard," Suzanne added quickly, feeling guilty over Neal's wife in some vague, unsettling way. She had, of course, heard the case against her adversary (rival? counterpart?); every small, mean, inexplicitly insensitive, consequential thing was laid out like so many steps, and she had trod on them all on her way to justification. Neal had seen to that. Then why hadn't he seen to the rest of it? The marriage was over, and yet the marriage went on and on. She had broken up nothing. Then was she guilty of nothing?

"It seems appropriate that it's Christmas," Beth said. She looked at her old friends. "I've always envied you two at Christmas."

Georgie glanced conspiratorially at Suzanne. "Isn't it time we told her the Yule truth?"

Suzanne shrugged. "Go ahead. Shatter an innocent."

"I know what you've been thinking, Beth. That without the perfect family you've missed out; it's amazing what power this holiday has, causing visions of sugarplums to dance in the heads of ordinarily sane, intelligent people." She leaned forward, warming to her subject. "But actually, Christmas is like having a baby: you forget the pain the moment it's over. Which is how the species has continued to propagate and how department stores have continued to profit. You walk around in a stupor every December, filled with giddy expectation—it feels so good, you know, the more kids the merrier, and presents are everywhere, everywhere! So you know you're part of it, this is the way it's supposed to be, you belong. That's what you imagined, didn't you? Belonging? A huge sparkling tree, children dressed in gorgeous innocence, turkey in the oven, relatives calling, peace on earth, all's right with the world?" Georgie had wound herself up in the telling, losing her way inadvertently, veering off from a mocking sarcasm to an inescapable truth.

"I'd sit there, looking at Lew. How could it be? I loved the kids almost crazily, flesh of my flesh and of his. Then I'd feel the crack coming up my center; that half of me, the woman half, dead." She looked at Beth. "Snap a picture-postcard life."

Beth winced, causing Georgie instant regret at having let such sharp disappointment spill out, when control had been her one grace note. It was as if she'd made a silent pact with her friends, one that recognized the inequity of complaining of something about which one had done nothing. It didn't matter why she stayed with Lew, not really, not in this instance. The salient fact was that she had rendered herself numb; why should they have to hear about it?

"And what were you doing all those Christmas mornings when you never would come to us? Imagining our familial perfection for a sentimental moment or two?" Suzanne asked, rescuing them.

"Making love," Beth said. "Well, what else do you do when you're not married and you don't have kids and it's Christmas?"

"Lew and I did that once," Georgie said, "I think it was the winter of sixty-three." But she was thinking of this other life she had never lived, more mysterious to her than she'd ever admit. It was an existence as familiar to Beth and Suzanne as the cadence of married life in the suburbs was to Georgie, but of course she knew that their boundaries were wider, their opportunities endless. Making love on Christmas morning, indeed; with this lover or that one, in this position or that one. Tom likes his eggs over easy, Dick eats bran, Harry takes his English muffins with marmalade; who could remember? You'd have to be a waitress to keep them all straight. So much better this way: one husband, one breakfast, one position.

"In all these years, have you ever taken anyone home?" Suzanne asked, referring to Beth's mother's house in Maryland.

"No one since Donald. I've kept up the ritual of going down there every year during the holidays, but never with an announcement in tow; that's how she'd see it. After Donald and I got divorced, my mother decided she liked him enormously."

"Maybe what she liked was what she perceived to be your safety. In retrospect, of course," Suzanne said, remembering Mrs. Taitlow's confounding, consuming censure of her daughter, the rather shocking specter of her ignoble reproach. She saw it now in Beth's eyes. "Or maybe it was just a mother underscoring her daughter's brinkmanship, unable to resist topping it with an exclamation point," she said. "In any event, ex-sons-in-law seem to have the edge"—a thought that prompted Georgie to wonder why her own mother persistently adored Lew.

They finished their meal in easy conversation, just the right note to achieve the momentary reprieve they sought. Lingering over coffee, they each felt unwilling to step back out into their lives quite yet. Suzanne found herself dreading the street, with its insistent reminders of holiday cheer; the sadness she suddenly felt was so heavy it seemed impossible she'd be able to stand up. It was deplorable, this situation of hers, of course it was, she knew it. But there was nothing for it right now, she knew that as well. The thing to do was to go home and paint, cover the canvas with colored tears. But she was not a Sunday painter, art was not her therapy; it was, in fact, part of her problem. Uneasy with the word "artist," which she thought presumptuous, she could manage, just barely, to refer to this tenuous, immaterial part of herself as a painter. What was it Dale had called her? An artist apocryphal, wielding her brush in the shadows. Too much about her was shadowy these days; why couldn't she take hold? She stole a look at Beth, as she often did, astonished yet again at her beauty, hardly diminished by the lines that had appeared. She was certain that the woman behind such a face knew things she would never know.

And all the while, Beth was wondering if time could stand still. But not now, not when despair was creeping through her body, spreading all over like the colored liquid they pour through you to illuminate your insides; a garish show. No; time, if it could have, should have stood still when she was twenty-seven. But then she'd have been stuck with the notion that babies and a man made the woman, whereas now she knew better: love your work, love yourself. Besides, there had always been men; there was Robert now. Exactly. Now. She felt as if she was floating, her skin already drawn into pruny slits from the water licking around her, bobbing like a bottle tossed carelessly to sea.

Finally, wishing each other a merry Christmas, they grabbed hands like children, their old gesture of solidarity, and held on tight. It infused them with the energy to make ready for the street, layered against the cold, faces in place.

Georgie watched Beth and Suzanne walk east in their stylish coats, certain they hadn't any idea what it was like to have run out of that housewife's staple, hope.

five

Remembering the havoc precipitated by Beth's pregnancy all those years ago, Suzanne found herself wondering what would happen if she herself was pregnant, right now, today—what would Neal do in these enlightened times if his mistress announced that their love child was hatching? She regretted her musing in a flash, for it seemed she knew precisely what Neal's reaction would be, even down to the words he'd use: "I love you more than anything in the world, and so we must have this child, keep this child, and we will all be together soon." They were tender, definitive words, lovely words, only words; Neal's weapons of choice.

Or perhaps she was being unfair. He'd mean what he said, absolutely. It was just that he was slow to act, and maddeningly unmoved by the price she paid as he ambled along. Poor at posing ultimatums, Suzanne had thought that her genuine distress would be lightning enough to cause this man who loved her to move mountains to bring her relief; at the very least, to get on with his divorce. Just how long did he think he could keep her coiled in a knot, watching her time on this earth roll by like a film with empty frames, irretrievable, overexposed?

Georgie had put that thought into her head, or, rather, pulled it from the recesses of her mind: "Soon we'll be old. Or *you'll* be old," she amended. "I don't intend to live that long." They had been talking about Neal, and Georgie had simply meant to point out that waiting was a young girl's game. Implicit in that, Suzanne thought, was the notion that only a girl (or a fool) would swallow the classic yarn about the man who's going to leave his wife any minute now, any hour, any day.

But then, how could others be expected to comprehend that her affair with Neal was different? That theirs was a bond that could not be viewed categorically, or measured in ordinary terms? Suzanne believed this even though she knew that everyone in love believed it; she saw her folly at the same time, just as everyone safely out of love saw it.

Of course when Beth was pregnant in 1960, being in love didn't matter one bit; only marriage mattered. And how persistently, how maddeningly that fetus had held on—through wild spurts of jumping, scalding baths, even fervent prayer: please God, just this one thing, *I'll never ask again*! But she had, they all had.

Still, it had strengthened them, this banding together at the height of Beth's desperation. For if they understood anything beyond the boundaries of their generation, the strictures that held them in muted order, it was that the friendship of women was a binding force, a specific solidity found nowhere else. It had given them the courage to stash Beth in a home for unwed mothers in Pennsylvania, where a sympathetic, perhaps illegally sensitive doctor promised utmost privacy and discretion. It had given them the canniness to provide the perfect alibi for Beth's absence the first half of their senior year: a semester in France—to which end Suzanne arranged for a mail drop through her cousin in Paris, satisfying Beth's parents with regular notes properly posted.

Most of all, it had given them that special sustenance that girlish intimacy portends: to be understood at last. They relied on it still, needing one another more than ever.

Suzanne had never seen Georgie so brittle beneath the folds of fat that could never sate, never mollify. Not even when Georgie had left Dennis the year after college had she seemed so overcome. Dennis, whom Georgie, young girl that she was, had ennobled with her adamant, slavish belief in his capacity for art, his ability to speak for a generation accused of having nothing to say. She chose to see his glumness as an aura, his selfishness as a necessity, her own devotion as his due. When finally Georgie awoke from her dream of being a great writer's Calliope, having gotten the wrong fellow who so ignobly wanted to shed *her,* it hurt so terribly she thought she'd die. It could be argued that she had. Suzanne often imagined that Georgie was actually buried under all that flesh, foreign stuff that somehow stuck to her frame and covered her over.

And Beth, turning out her columns with a steady hand, educating, elucidating, illuminating, without apparent exertion. She said of herself, derisively, that she was a font of small ideas, but she said it only to Suzanne and Georgie, and only because they knew her naked self so well she figured they were as incredulous as she was at her success. The trouble was, she couldn't write her life. Now this latest man who shared it, Robert, was away for Christmas; Suzanne could tell it was the beginning of the end, she saw it in Beth's face. And she knew that when Beth and Robert were no longer living together her old friend would not slide into a funk of sadness: not over *him.* This was not a woman whose heart broke. Not anymore.

And here am I, she thought, waiting for Neal to give me my life. Oh, I know what you meant, Georgie, split up the center. For I do exist, of course I exist. I love and care for my children, I create the work I am paid to do and occasionally even excel at it; I function. But the woman half lies in wait, separate, aching. I hate the powerlessness I feel as I hold out for this man to—what? Make me real? Give me value? I despise having remained that pathetic thing I was brought up to be: denizen of a sub-class meant only for joining; useless, worthless alone. I stand here, the epitome of the women's movement—self-realized, self-actualized, self-deluded. A flaw in my nature, surely.

Now she heard Annie, her nine-year-old, singing a song that Neal had taught her. She sang it mindlessly as she worked a puzzle, and Suzanne remembered the day, the very moment when it had been absolutely too late to turn back:

"Boom boom didum dadum whadat . . ." Neal had nodded to Annie:

"Chew!"

"Boob boom didum dadum whadat . . ."

"This is stupid." Daniel's turn.

"Chew!"

"And they fam and they fam all . . ."

"Over de land."

"Over de land." Neal, putting a cap on it.

He paused, sipped his Scotch. Suddenly his body jerked and he sang again, seemingly involuntarily, "over de land." A moment later without warning he jerked again: "over de land." Annie squealed, watching now, waiting.

He had pulled a cigarette from his pack, tapped it on the arm of the chair, ran his fingers over it, took out his lighter, lit the cigarette, puffed at it, inhaled, and slowly, with great concentration, his mouth a perfect oval, blew out the smoke. He puffed again, feigning innocence, nonchalance, Annie holding her stare, holding it, holding it. Neal looking around the room now, over her, under her, beside her, his eyes curiously examining absolutely nothing, stretching her string until finally her attention flagged a fraction. And in that instant his shoulders shuddered as if seized by a spasm: "over de land."

"Get the hook," Daniel said, pleased with his knowledge of the old vaudeville solution for a bad act. Annie giggled, then sobered up, signaling Neal to go on with the game.

Surveying all this from the kitchen, her seat for so many scenes from her life, Suzanne saw Annie on the floor near Neal's feet and knew at once her daughter's desire to be warm in his lap, and her reticence to chance it; she saw Daniel leaning against a wall, a book in the hands he didn't know what to do with, and felt in her twelve-year-old's awkward stance his wanting to be part of everything and his fear of measuring up. They were so needy, so very much her children. Hadn't she a closet full of clothes to prove it?

"Fear clothes, that's all I've got here," she had explained to Dale, in those days after her divorce when she was dressing for her second life, hoping she might still need her heart.

"*You* know, you've been in a dry spell long enough to be nearly convinced you really are unwanted and unloved; then, suddenly, you're invited to a party. Naturally, apprehension grabs you by the throat so you run out and buy something you can't afford, something casual, you know? It's got to look casual, like you barely had time to throw it together but when you did it just happened to look gorgeous because what if *he's* there, the one you don't need to meet? Then in the dressing room, with those sadistic lights, you find out your hair has no luster and your laugh lines are not funny, and when you see the zit on your chin you think, what is this, prom night? You buy the stuff anyway and tuck it hopefully under your arm like a transformation kit from a God willing at least to humor you. Then your child gets sick or your sitter backs out and you can't even go, or you *do* go and there is absolutely no one there but other hungry people to whom it is out of the question you would ever be attracted. Either way, into the closet they go, those emblems of your vulnerability, to hang there in shame."

Suzanne looked across the table at Neal, her good fortune. He was diving into his steak, the steam from his baked potato checked by a glob of sour cream, no green on his plate.

"Honey, eat your broccoli," Suzanne had said.

"Yuchh." Annie shivered with disgust.

"Annie."

"I can't! I'll throw up."

Annie received the mother look and might have taken a tentative stab at the broccoli if Neal hadn't said, succinctly, "green turd."

Daniel and Annie looked at him, then at Suzanne, who turned the mother look on Neal and tried to hold it. But he was chewing a huge piece of steak with great deliberation, his mouth primly closed, looking directly at her glazed eyes; she burst out laughing.

"Know how you get rosy cheeks?" Annie said.

"You rub beets on them," Daniel said.

"*I* wanted to tell it!"

"Mom hated beets, and when Grandma said she had to eat them to get rosy cheeks . . ."

"We get the picture," Suzanne said. "And just when did Grandma snitch?"

Annie perked up. "She always snitches. One time she told us you . . ."

"Nev-ver mind," Suzanne said, stopping nothing.

While the children slept, Suzanne and Neal lay side-by-side on the couch, its pillows on the floor.

"She wants me to come back tomorrow," Neal said.

"Annie? She said that?"

"Umm." He held her, felt her burrowing in with gratefulness, relief. "In case you have cauliflower."

They lay there quietly, lulled by their perfection, in these last moments before Neal had to leave. Suzanne secretly worried over Daniel; what would Neal have in his grab bag for Daniel? But he would have something, she knew he would; Neal had the deepest bag she had ever seen. In just two months, with indefatigable energy, he had carved out a place for Annie that the child recognized and would, Suzanne knew, soon occupy. But her boy, who remembered more and healed slowly, would not be so easily led. Daniel felt betrayed by his parents' divorce, that inanimate thing, that action that had taken his father away. Neal could neither replace him, nor convincingly prove his own fidelity—not to Daniel.

All that summer she had a picture in her mind of her children's rush to embrace this conveyer of their mother's joy, bowled over by the sheer weight of his good intentions. Forgetting that they were people, each weaving different patterns separate from hers. Having no idea that Neal, childless, would take them on as clients, attending the surface with a dazzle that merely caused them, initially, to blink. She had wanted them to be lovable, acceptable, her pride all wound up in them as if they were a gift she had fashioned herself. And so she had defended, explained, until he stopped her. What was she doing? He understood; they were wonderful, it just needed time, and they had the time, all the time in the world, their whole lives. Annie expected a goodnight kiss from him now, and he had begun cautiously venturing into Daniel's room in search of a bond. The room was bare, Daniel obdurate. And still Neal went back, and back.

"Hi," Neal said softly, and reached for her, kissed her. Oh urgent urgent kisses, and no time. "See what you do to me?" She saw. He pulled away, heaved a deep sigh. "I have to . . ."

"I know," she said.

"I love you. So much." They gazed at each other, half smiles on their faces, every crease, every line momentarily smoothed, certain they hadn't uttered simple lies. Then Neal lit a cigarette, his normal preparation for the street, and got his coat. Where did you tell her you were going, Suzanne thought, what makes this the hour you have to get back? She always wondered, never asked. Just as she never asked, "When are you going to leave your wife?" He held her, told her he'd call her early in the morning, blew a kiss from the elevator, and was gone.

She had felt whole then, her skin had had the beatific glow of a true believer. His marriage would end, and their inexorable connection would have its destined life.

"It's going exactly right now," Neal had said at their Monday lunch.

"Is it?"

"Yes."

It was understood that this would hold her, though it had already become part of their love patter: sweet-sounding, meaningless. Knowing this but not acknowledging it, Neal had looked furtively around the restaurant, hamming it up for her pleasure, then had leaned over and kissed her. End of scene. For she didn't require specifics, that was the wonder of it: she intuited him, his very being, read between the lines, filled in the blanks with the best of him; he always said that.

He was still saying it. She was still wondering where he'd gotten it from. She had only been herself, done only what she knew, and this man had come upon her as if discovering a rare flower of exquisite grace, received her words, her thoughts, with awe, touched her, drank from her trembling, and pronounced her peerless. And expected no less.

She had gone from the blush of surprise and embarrassment at his view of her to dependency upon it. Now, if she was not who he said she was, who was she? And why would he love her?

The trouble was, nothing had happened.

Nothing.

Absolutely nothing.

He was still with his wife. It was still going "exactly right." And Suzanne felt herself adrift from that aerie where the atmosphere was uncommonly pure, merely up too high now for her own good.

six

Beth had started early enough, as if she knew that her body, her face, her hair and everything in her closet would let her down. Bizarre ritual of women, dressing for a party.

She hated parties, that was it. Especially on New Year's Eve. And so she'd stashed a bottle of Piper-Heidsieck in the refrigerator, along with their favorite sesame chicken from the gourmet shop, in the faint hope that Robert would, at the very last moment, peel off his tux and the new skin he'd grown and insist they stay home, regardless. Regardless of the fact that Robert was now among the charmed, the inner circle, invited to his company president's home for the annual black-tie dinner. Another bizarre ritual wherein the chosen trek to a sprawling, indistinct house to pay homage to a balding Midwestern Protestant with straight white teeth and the instincts of Orka, his pert wife, two dumb dogs and three good corporate children who could wipe the sullenness off their faces in one threatening wink, and did.

She surveyed the havoc she had already wreaked: dresses flung about, discarded, Rorschach-like blotches created by the desperation of an adolescent. She'd planned what she was going to wear, but it had looked wretched, she'd known it instantly and panicked. Why hadn't she bought a new dress, why did she do this to herself, why did she hold out, obstinate, superior, determined not to be dragged into this maze? Why didn't she know it would take hold of her now, this desire to make a good impression, to be exactly right, the obvious reality of judgment. What did she know of business anyway? She who merely wrote about the cynical excesses of corporations and cartels, what did she know of the language and customs of this subculture, the nuances of civilized warfare, the booty at stake? She'd witnessed only the lower levels, the gossipmongering and oily maneuvering in the bullpen at the *Herald,* before her column was syndicated. All right then, all right, Robert was one of the "big boys" now, as he liked to put it under the cover of night, covering it further with a boyish laugh, fooling neither of them. She'd do her part, then, she'd do it, find a mask, paint it on. For Robert, who trusted her with his secrets.

She was wearing green silk when the phone rang.

"Hey Beth, Bobby there?"

As Robert reached for the phone and took her in, a breathy "whoo" sound came from his lips, which was, she thought, entirely open to interpretation. But not hers. Who was this "Bobby"? As we play more serious games, do we adopt more childish names? She remembered the good old boys who tromped in and out of her father's house in Bethesda, many of them hold-overs from her grandfather's day, senators, congressmen, wily killers with little-boy names, the Billys, the Joe Bobs.

She listened, fascinated, as "Bobby" fired one-liners into the phone in a foreign male shorthand, his back an unyielding mass, his right foot tapping to his success, his arrival. She was not surprised by his eager embrace of it, nor did she for a moment begrudge it. What hung there between them was the shift in their balancing act. Eerily, the classic syndrome of successful husband, wife left behind, marriage gone amok flashed through her head, as if she had never clearly understood it before. But she wasn't his wife, nor a housewife at all; successful in her own right when they had met nearly two years before, *she* was the one who was one of the big boys, she was the one who had made it. Or so he said. She'd been charmed by his delight in her accomplishments, his genuine respect, and later, when they were joined, his pride. It had never occurred to her to measure herself as he did. She worked hard; she knew her writing was acceptable, she even knew the luxury of an occasional phrase or paragraph that took her, momentarily, beyond what she knew, deep down, to be her limitations. But she did not view her work in terms of a pecking order, the ranking of a life. Robert told her this was because she'd never worked for a corporation in the usual sense, as a nine-to-five employee: that she'd never suffered the indignity of handing over to someone else the decision of what she was worth. She had, of course; there had always been editors and a constituency that would either accept or reject her work. But she believed in the value, the legitimacy of her own measure. Robert said the independently wealthy and the exceptionally talented could afford to impress themselves, that this had nothing whatever to do with regular people. Even exceptional regular people.

When Robert got off the phone he told her she looked beautiful, he smiled but did not touch her and went off to shower. It was the automatic smile of a man otherwise engaged in manly things, who knew what was expected and would remember to comply.

When they had met she had been working on a column about computers, at a time when whiz kids were committing semicriminal acts with this new toy, tapping into credit cards and even the corridors of power, while their elders, like Beth, were dazed by a technology they doubted their ability to grasp. She had gotten to Robert's company through a friend; Robert had been the one dispatched to give her a mini-education because of his ability to isolate and impart what she needed to know and not a drop beyond it. It was the art of a supersalesman, yet Robert was hardly slick in Beth's presence. In fact he seemed boyish and tentative, and that, coupled with his knowledge of a discipline that to Beth was futuristic and even slightly foreboding . . . not to mention pure Greek . . . appealed to her. In the midst of their third conversation he blurted out how difficult it was to be so awfully attracted to someone and unable to do anything about it. "Oh, I'm so sorry," she said, "a war wound?" His mouth had hung open for an instant, and then he burst out laughing, this bundle of corporate nerves who had assumed she was a personal friend of the head of his company, perhaps close enough to carry tales, even judgments. She didn't see that then, it didn't register in the glow of her initial attraction; when it did it was too late.

She hadn't hated parties when she was Robert's talisman, his prize. He'd even brought her to his father as proof of his worth, ticking off her accomplishments, the column carried nationwide, the collection of her best pieces published three years ago, with a second edition already planned. And need he mention her astonishing aura, those breasts, that hair? Oh, he paraded her shamelessly, like some exotic species, a plumed beauty that could think, too! And all of it was merely to say, I must be deserving, see who loves me! She heard it, heard that singsong whiny child's voice ringing out so painfully around them as she sat for inspection, bearer of such tenuous satisfaction. Until his promotion catapulted him beyond his father's mean predictions.

Robert was out of the bathroom and she went in, wiped the mirror and worked at her face, trying to make it look familiar. Her armpits felt sweaty, the steam had taken the curl out of her hair. She sat on the edge of the tub as she had all those years ago when she was pregnant, wanting to run far away, to erase and start again. But this was the "again"; how was it possible that it came so soon, why wasn't she ready? The face of Dennis Mayo appeared from years of blankness with such stunning clarity it took her breath away and caused her to sway off balance and grab at the sink. Dennis. The boy Georgie had loved, the boy with whom Beth had betrayed her. She had immediately disremembered his touch, disavowed it; had released herself from him, and ultimately from his baby inside her.

Moments passed as she fought the pictures that rose in her mind, each giving birth to another, a horrid gaggle of unforgiveness. And she succeeded. She was a grown woman with years of practice at finding the "off" button. She finished her face, decorated the package with just the right jewels, sweetened it with just enough perfume, and presented it for inspection with a modest glow of anticipation.

And Robert was pleased. This stranger she was living with who hoisted his own sails now, who was propelled by his own wind, his face puffed with self-elation, attending nothing outside his own hard-won glow beyond the expedient—Robert was pleased.

seven

The idea of suicide had come to Georgie before. She'd only flirted with it as a possible backup, and never at a moment of great drama; perhaps because there hadn't been any. Lew's affair, once Georgie had discovered it, had left him sodden with grief and remorse. And while Georgie had been forgiving, it was more as an acceptance of her part in a traditional play than a struggle to overcome a feeling of betrayal or despair.

That was two years ago. The "other woman" had been a secretary at his law firm who always looked as if she'd just stuck her gum under the desk. Thin, though. Young, and thin. Georgie knew it wasn't serious; rather it was a ritual stopover for a man rounding his fiftieth corner. She'd had the good sense not to press it. In Georgie's eyes, hers was a marriage that was as inevitable as it was flat, but it allowed her to carve out a separate place where she could hide and brood with no one the wiser. She needed to preserve that place; it was all she knew. And in fact there'd never been any real danger: Lew loved her. She responded meagerly, a fact she hated to admit even to herself, but then Lew seemed to expect so little, and received what she thought of as her scraps with gratitude. It was a pattern they'd fallen into early on; was that her fault?

No, there had been no drama, and that had been the point. Fresh out of college she had plunged into the chaos that was Dennis Mayo, where Georgie had been the lover, the receiver of scraps. She'd had her heart broken thoroughly, and emerged with a profound belief in the mundane, having finally understood there was no other safe place. She had embraced Lew as the numbing instrument he promised to be, and had not been disappointed. If at times her passion rose up from that deep place where she'd stuffed it, nerve ends like thousands of fine pins pricking at her skin, invisible raw red patches traveling down her arms, her breasts, her belly, it wasn't Lew's fault. Nor had she given in to it. She'd harnessed every raging itch with the cool eye of a survivor, distilling it, redirecting it to anything at hand: her home, her clothes, her cooking, her façade. And so they said Georgie had élan. Georgie was different, but not too different; Georgie was their resident character, counted upon to poke at their normalcy, stretch their common restraints, depended upon not to go too far.

The trouble was she had become certifiably crazy in the process, or so she believed. Who but a crazy person would dive into lukewarm water and *stay* under, resisting risk, passion, feeling? Oh, the children, yes, she'd had all of that, nor could she dismiss it. She'd loved them well, gotten them through, set them free. They were gone now. When she and Lew had taken Shawn, the last one, the baby, to college in the fall, Shawn had urged them to leave as quickly as possible, embarrassed by their presence, their very existence. Well. She understood. Hadn't she been through it twice before? And hadn't she done the same to her own parents, all those years ago? Of course. She waited for that feeling of loss to overtake her, for the disorientation, the emptiness her friends spoke of to seep through her pores and plunge her into depression. But she felt nothing. The house was quiet, lifeless now, yet she'd never been fooled, never been taken in by her own creation. What was this house so carefully draped if not a visible extension of her inner self?

Suicide, then, was something she mused upon over the years, merely as an alternative to a fabricated life. But the years had gone by, and she had survived them. And while she liked to think she took death lightly, being one of those people who understood the futility of life, there was the time her car had swerved out of control on the ice and she'd struggled wildly to right it, to save herself. The children had been with her and it was out of the question that she would let harm befall them. Yet it had been her own life she had thought of, in that split second. She was younger then, and, looking back, she imagined she must have had some vague sense of possibilities, although what they might have been she couldn't guess. She hadn't been forced into her life, she had consciously chosen it, chosen Lew. She had no brief against anyone, except perhaps Dennis—but then who among the living hadn't had their heart broken by someone? Was it his fault that Georgie had snapped, and never snapped back?

The truth was, everything had gone as planned—on the larger scale. What Georgie hadn't reckoned on was the feeling, stronger than ever now, that she was slipping away. She imagined herself being sucked down an ordinary drain, or melting, right on the spot, her blue housecoat in need of a cleaning left there in a clump, a final embarrassment.

A psychiatrist told her that she ate because she was still mad at her father; another said it was Lew's affair, coming at the heels of an empty nest, food a replacement for love. She could have said, what do *they* know? But then, what did she tell them? Even in those low-lit dens with their boxes of Kleenex at the ready and deep chairs of inviting worn leather, she couldn't resist playing the ham. One psychiatrist had eventually thrown up his hands and thrown her out, when she led him down the fanciful path of her husband, the secret transvestite. Another one found her too amusing to let go. Or perhaps he hoped to unravel her with patience. Georgie, for her part, wanted to believe that she was doing something constructive for herself and in her usual destructive fashion made sure she didn't succeed. She could see that now. She could see it from the moment memory had exploded, on the telephone in her kitchen, and the pieces of her old self came floating down: Georgie back there at Carlisle University, a girl in the throes of willfully romantic love.

"Dennis wants me to go with him, he wants me to go!" George had announced, breathless, having run all the way back to the dorm. Suzanne and Beth had hugged her, jumping up and down until they all collapsed on the floor in a heap.

Suzanne's eyes were wide. "Are you getting married?" Not a question that normally needed to be asked in 1961, when a senior was going clear across country to live with the man she loved. But this was Dennis Mayo, spiritual kin to Cornell's Farina, self-proclaimed intimate of Ferlinghetti and Ginsberg, Judy Collins's muse.

"Who knows! Who cares!" Ah, indeed. She did care, of

course, no matter how hard she had tried to follow the beat, no matter how fervently she had said she believed in it. She wanted Dennis, wanted to have him, hold him, keep him, and that meant marriage. Marriage was forever.

This marriage lasted six months. They made their way to California slowly, in his old black Ford, clad themselves in the ritual black. The first few days Georgie's face was flushed, nearly emblazoned from the slap she knew her father would have given her had he not had to settle for screaming invectives over the telephone, and the boldness of her deaf ear, the finality of it. They veered off to make her Mrs. Mayo; Georgie had been cool, deft, engineering that stopover with a fine hand as the car creaked and moaned. And if her good ear definitely picked up that, for Dennis, marriage was something to be tried, like Turkish cigarettes, or working, her pale butterfly lips never uttered a bourgeois word of it. They were free, free! Dennis to write, she to encourage and inspire, lusting for nothing but truth and each other.

True, she hadn't expected an audience. But Dooley and Leo opened their doors and took them in until they could get settled in a place of their own, and somehow they never did. Dennis introduced her as "my lady," which charged her up with the same exquisite joy it had when he first said it, when they'd first made love: "You're my lady now." No mere girlfriend she, but her man's lady. She loved it.

The house, a three-story brownstone on Telegraph Hill in San Francisco, was Leo's, given him by his parents with the understanding that they'd pay his bills if he kept his distance. As added insurance, his family lived primarily in Europe, venturing only as close as New York for a few months each year. The checks came like clockwork, no notes attached, payoffs to this bizarre homosexual "son" whom the gods had wished upon them, surely, in a moment of misdirected malice. On occasion, Leo would rip up one of the checks and flush it down the toilet, and because the fancy struck him when he was drunk, which was often, and when there was a suitably appreciative audience, which could be any time, those who were dependent upon that check had to watch him zealously. And that included Dooley, Dennis, Georgie, and a group of indolent, would-be intellectuals Georgie dubbed "the North Beach Fleet."

They hung around Leo's bookstore, which he called "Bloom" although his name was Blum, for its constant supply of coffee, sweet rolls, grass, Mars bars and poets. And for Fiona, who would not speak but sang her thoughts in a quivering soprano that made them shiver for its delicacy and unexpected strength. Fiona sang of love and death, which seemed to cover it all, her long blond hair like a shimmering halo, the curiously flat Scandinavian face betraying nothing. Her body was difficult to find under the layers of jumpers and sweaters she always wore; her appeal went beyond sex to a promise of warm, cave-like apertures in which a man could get lost. When Fiona sang, Georgie's hand invariably found its way to Dennis's knee, in ownership as much as love. Still, Fiona came and went only with Charles, as black as she was pale, and presumably, on occasion, she broke her silence with him.

If Georgie was stunned at first to find that Dennis was not the resident God he had been on the fringes of Carlisle University, holding court in an off-campus coffeehouse with the cachet that comes of no longer being a student, she got over it. He did belong here, they did welcome him as one of their own, and while his rank in the order of things was somewhat diminished—Leo was king, understandably, and Dooley, having published a poem in *Partisan Review,* was literary prince—in Georgie's eyes Dennis was the magic man who would one day outdistance them all. And though she feigned nonchalance, her Midwestern heart was thrilled at the magnitude of her escape. She was Dennis Mayo's lady now, intimate of Leo Blum, the cast-off son and North Beach legend, of Dooley at the beginning, before the moment, of Fiona and Charles and the whole underside world that was hatching. She was there!

Her father was in Wheaton, paying for cashmere sweater sets for her sisters whom he claimed to be his only children. She felt no remorse, only pity, a vast well of pity for everyone in the endless dark, unaware of the roaring wave that was coming.

Then, imperceptibly at first, Dennis began to wind down. He'd written fitfully at Carlisle, disappearing for two or three days at a time and then producing a few pages of his novel for her greedy eyes. Still, she'd never been conscious of prolonged inactivity; there seemed to be a rhythm to Dennis's creative spurts. But here he slept late, lazed around, idled over at the Beach, ate her communal dinners, drank through the evening, made love, and slept again. Then there began to be spaces between their lovemaking. He'd skip Tuesday or Thursday or two days in a row and she would feel her body shrivel beside him.

She tried to get him to work, delicately at first, aware of the fragility of such a divine function, and she got nowhere. But she was not a weak girl, not in the end a trembler, and when she felt Dennis slipping away, his art and his ardor drying up, she fought. Dennis finally holed himself up somewhere for nearly a week, and flung finished pages at her in scornful triumph when he returned. She read them, and recognized them, and soon it all became clear. He hadn't written a word in two years. All the time she had known him at Carlisle, he had fed her page after page of what he'd already written. He just forgot where he left off, and gave her repeats by mistake. He had sixty-seven pages in all.

He went berserk when she found him out, blaming her with the logic of the culpable: she'd drained him with her cloying, her fawning, her middle-class constipation; he needed air, room, freedom! To her own surprise, Georgie hurled back that he was a phony; if he wanted air, room and freedom why did he live off Leo and live in Leo's house? He had slapped her then, very hard, across the face. And seemed as startled as she was, and rocked her in his arms.

They made love as if they might break, and fell asleep exhausted. And for the next several days she had her Dennis back, the one with whom she'd fallen so madly in love, who would sit with her under the stars and point a stubby finger at Ursa Minor and Lyra and Corona Borealis, who savored Greek mythology and told its tales so well as to be spellbinding, only to leap from Poseidon and Orpheus and Sisyphus to wicked parodies of MGM musicals, Patti Page and Johnnie Ray.

It didn't last. The week he had disappeared he'd been with Fiona; Charles hadn't minded, why should she? He gave her a list of his infidelities as if he'd been suddenly injected with truth serum: Carol, Mary, Eve. Gretchen he actually brought home, to the delight of Leo, who loved drama, and Dooley, who shared her. As much as Georgie tried to emulate the much-heralded Gretchen, to be loose, casual, a free spirit of mysterious calm, she was a Wheaton girl after all, who damn well wanted her husband for herself and was mortified by his blatant disregard.

Gretchen was a large-breasted girl with alabaster skin and

the countenance of a zombie, who called everyone "man," including Georgie. She wanted the three of them to make love as a symbol of universal oneness and the death of middle-class bullshit. It was only inertia, she said, that kept those few among their parents' generation pure; the rest played their dirty games behind closed doors and then went to church on Sunday. Georgie had heard it all before, why did it suddenly sound so tinny? Half the people on the Beach were stoned more than half the time, yet Gretchen's trances seemed contrived for effect, as did everything about Gretchen. Georgie knew the girl was a kook who would fly away at a moment's notice, but it couldn't be soon enough, and it wasn't. Free of her at last, Georgie was left with nothing to filter the unraveling of her marriage. There only remained the scenes that Leo relished, until at last even he got uneasy.

Still Georgie couldn't let go. The defeat was too overwhelming, and the harder she held to it, to Dennis, the more violently he struggled to throw her off. She seemed to be in a trance herself now, prowling the empty house by day, confused because what she had thought to be artful charm now appeared to be perpetual squalor. She continued to cook sumptuous meals, even if they were always built around pasta and rice, and everyone came home for them, even Dennis. Dooley would bring a woman, or go off to his room to work. But Leo, whose house was open to all, remained alone, their audience. They rarely disappointed him.

Once, in a discourse on spaghetti, Dooley informed them that the one certain way to know if it was *al dente* was to throw a sliver or two against the wall and see if it stuck; within seconds the meal she'd slaved over was hurled all over the kitchen. When tears sprang to Georgie's eyes, Dooley, still laughing, wiped at them gently and offered to go out for a pizza. But Dennis, suddenly railing at her housewife mentality, grabbed the colander from the sink and poured the remaining spaghetti over her head. There was nothing for it but to laugh, and she did laugh, with the uneasiness of the good sport whose trial may not be over. Dennis hugged her, and rubbed some of the spaghetti onto his own head. They washed each other off in the shower and made love giddily. Then Dennis went with Dooley for the pizza and didn't return until the following night.

She had no idea how long it went on like this, Dennis throwing her crumbs of his old self every now and then. He sat up with her the night she had cramps and soothed her by reading e.e. cummings aloud, hating the poet himself but knowing that Georgie loved him. "Cummings is like a tittering schoolgirl who dots her i's with circles," Dennis said, making her feel a fool, because in truth, mud-luscious and puddle wonderful was what she had thought her life would be. Occasionally the old banter would surface, Dooley asking in what he thought to be Freud's plaintive whine, "What do women want?" and Dennis, a cool O. Henry, would reply "Why, whatever you're out of!" And in quieter moments, Dooley quoted Yeats, his and Georgie's favorite. Yet when he recited "tread softly because you tread on my dreams" she thought her wounded heart would break.

Dennis paid no attention; it seemed the more she felt, the less he noticed, until Georgie no longer knew how to behave. He was blatant with his women now, rubbing her nose in it on the one hand, on the other telling her it meant nothing at all; he borrowed shamelessly from Leo with no intention of paying him back: what did money *mean,* after all? Yet when Leo, in one of his fits of indignation, ripped a check ceremoniously over the toilet, it was Dennis who fished out all the pieces, dried them carefully, even lovingly, Georgie thought, and taped them together with the fine hand of an artist, while Leo cried.

She had spent that day, a Sunday, attacking the house like a whirling dervish. She had opened all the windows, changed the sheets, scrubbed, dusted, vacuumed, polished and felt, in the process, as if she had been reborn. It would be all right now. She had awakened knowing precisely what to do.

What could have possessed her? She still wondered, could still envision the checked tablecloth swiped from somewhere along the way, the candles, the matching dishes, how had she managed that? "Mrs. Robinson" in the background, artichokes vinaigrette, fresh pompano, Caesar salad, betraying the upper-middle-class cook of renown she'd become! And what did she have in what Dennis dubbed her "celebrated circle-pin mind" if not—what else?—a baby. That was the answer to everything, wasn't it?

She'd managed all these years not to conjure it up, her genuine *Reader's Digest* Most Embarrassing Moment, yet here it was, here it was. Dennis had walked into a spotless house and decided not to notice. He ate everything that was put in front of him and was still hungry when the meal was over; had she invented *nouvelle cuisine* without knowing it? She smiled until her face hurt, just as she had done in eighth grade when Dickie van Sant said her smile was beautiful. She had served her lover as one would a king, then cleared the debris to make way for espresso, cheap sherry and a paean to parenthood. Dennis, having satisfied himself that he'd heard what he thought he had heard, began a raucous rendition of the Kingston Trio's "Man Who Never Returned," pausing intermittently to laugh wildly and to gasp for air.

Naturally it was Georgie's job to take precautions, Dennis being philosophically opposed to prophylactics. Now he vowed he'd never touch her again, claiming she could no longer be trusted. He was right, of course. Then why had she tipped her hand, why? Because she believed in the magic of babies, and the destiny she was bred for.

Her father received her unceremoniously, while her mother, who kept her Kappa pin in a safe-deposit box, dispensed sunshine with fluttering hands and good intentions. An annulment was arranged with dispatch. Georgie took to parties and plaid with a vengeance. Within a year she was married to Lew.

Dennis? Dennis who?

eight

Robert lay beside Beth in deep sleep, exhausted from love-making. No. Exhausted from every other thing he had done that day and every day before it, now that he turned to work for sustenance; its power fueled him, it energized every cell within him, it was too much for her. She could not do it battle; she would lose. Had, in fact, lost already, and she knew it. She thought that it should matter more; that her life, other than her work, should require something more of her than to walk through invisible doors and emerge untouched, unscathed.

She had feigned desire as much as he had, she with the reflexive woman's act of holding on, he from lack of courage to admit their defeat. He had no need for her anymore—and yet it should not be based on need after all, should it? Not today. She could never keep it straight, but she knew enough about the era in which she lived to know that need was, well

. . . so seventies. Back then, relationships were presumably made and marriages saved by sex manuals with pictures; in these times, mind fucking was the thing. Beth wondered if it would ever be possible to sort out the layers of her own rationalizing from those she had so readily absorbed from each generation in her lifetime. A compendium of human inanity? Perhaps just collective frailty.

Right at this moment, trying to concentrate as she looked at Robert, her "significant other" in this decade of the eighties, Beth saw a male blob, its mouth slightly open, its rhythmic breathing interrupted, at odd beats, by low rasping sounds. She felt neither love nor hate nor even disappointment. Who was he? She hadn't the vaguest idea; the wind had blown it all away.

Three weeks had passed since her luncheon with Georgie and Suzanne, and in that time Beth had recognized that the focus of her life had shifted. What had once seemed so important, the tenor of her connection with Robert, had slipped away—just as the pregnancy she had feared, Robert's child, had slipped away; silently, undramatically.

But her life had always centered on work and a man, whichever man. She was well acquainted with the void left when love, or what she had wished or willed to be love, broke into pieces or slowly eroded; that curious mixture of displacement and deliverance, relief and regret. She knew what it was like to be alone with her typewriter—friend, enemy; unforgiving, relentless appendage that gave such niggling joy. This was different.

Self-absorption, Beth's periodic malaise and, she knew, an especially odious one when it got out of hand, seemed to have had her cornered these last several weeks: a relationship falling apart, then the fear of pregnancy; what more? But more came—the past came back, triggered by its possible recurrence.

She had given up a baby, handed her over and run as one would from a pinless grenade; she had never looked back, so eager was she for a clean slate, a life unencumbered. Her body had healed and her mind had cooperated, closing the door, sealing it tight. Over the years she'd had no other brushes with motherhood, and so she remained in a state of denial that was easily maintained—until the moment pregnancy again loomed as a possibility, flooding her consciousness with the stunning revelation that while she had given up a baby, she wasn't rid of her; that this fact of her life was fixed, central.

She could still see herself walking across campus at Carlisle University, through the archways and on into Collegetown, down the steep hill toward the Elixir, her toes curling into the sidewalk, a slight breeze, her nipples hard. She had told Suzanne she was looking for Georgie; in fact she had seen Georgie mounting the library steps, her shoulders hunched from the weight of the books she was carrying, so many nights with Dennis, so much catching up to do. Then Beth had slipped into that dark cave, the Elixir coffeehouse, and peered around innocently for the friend who wasn't there. She turned to leave, and then tilted her head as if caught by the music, drawn to it, straining to find its source. Her eyes lit on Dennis and she hugged her arms, willing him to sense her presence. "And who but my Lady Greensleeves?"; who would not be pulled into that sound? And so he sang it to her, that last verse, expecting her after all.

Donald, the boy she would eventually marry, was what she'd been brought up to expect. Donald, who would pet with her wildly but never press her beyond, who would never dream she had it in her to crash through that protective barrier designed to keep her safe from *him.* And yet, probably she wouldn't have. Not with Donald. Not with a boy in chinos and crew neck and scuffed white ducks, with good study habits and a future preordained. That was her fate, not to be tampered with; she knew the rules. But she longed for . . . what? Danger? It wasn't that she didn't love Donald: she loved him within the full range of her understanding of the fitness of things, with groping excitement and sweet familiarity and dreams of just deserts. But Dennis didn't play by rules, didn't even recognize them. She could experiment with Dennis and remain, within her own circle, even within her own head, the girl she was supposed to be. Never thinking, for a moment, she'd pay with a life.

She let Georgie and Suzanne believe that Donald was the father of the child. They had naturally assumed it, and she, in the eye of the storm, convinced herself it was right that they believe it, right that they not know of her betrayal, sleeping with Georgie's Dennis. Especially right that she not have to suffer their censure, their wrath, when she so desperately needed their indomitable support to stay afloat.

Beth shivered, thinking of it all these years later. She was astonished at how many lives she seemed to have lived since then, how well she'd covered her duplicity so that it wasn't only Georgie and Suzanne who didn't know; she herself had forgotten it long ago. One night with Dennis, Georgie's Dennis—that couldn't be the end of the world, could it? And then when it could, it very well could—when she was pregnant with Dennis's child—she couldn't face it, she was overcome by the fearful, practical matter at hand.

Later, of course, it hadn't been hard to convince herself that with Georgie safely married to Lew, she to Donald and Suzanne to Mark, with real life having finally descended upon them—what did it matter? Childish things best laid to rest in that first plunge into adulthood. They had homes, husbands, babies, dinner parties! They had sunk right into it, as programmed. Then suddenly the sixties' kids broke rank and rushed to tear it all apart, leaving the grown-up kids that directly preceded them dazed at having joined the enemy before the battle lines had been drawn, feeling cheated. Dennis Mayo had no platform, no politics; it was adolescence drawn out, as it was with most of the rebels they knew. Yet it had seemed daring then to be directionless, a sign of depth to appreciate jazz, and you couldn't know all of Woody's songs without being on the side of the angels. It's your land and mine all right, but when it's time to buy a house, find a good white neighborhood. . . . Well. They'd deprogrammed themselves to some degree, some of them, and then woke up in the foreground of women's liberation, actually changing society when the roar of the sixties had turned to dust, hobbled institutions its legacy.

The women in my life.

She pulled on a pair of jeans and a sweater and was nearly out the door when Robert woke up.

"Where are you going?"

"For a walk."

"Are you crazy?" He squinted at the clock. "It's twelve-fifteen."

She buttoned her coat. He lit a cigarette, hauling himself up for The Conversation, so long overdue. And she knew that, with her mind and heart diverted, he would be confused and she more desirable. It was for men to be silent, not women. She was to pour her heart out, careful to speak only of effect, not cause; he was to make his explanations plausible enough and promise to pay more attention, be more considerate—after which he'd continue doing exactly what he had been doing, exactly as he pleased, preparatory to the final confrontation, when she would feel forced to force the issue. And she thought, my God, I've been around the track so many times I can write each scene in advance.

She saw the weight of his goodness on his shoulders, the willingness to listen and respond to her female plaint in the middle of the night before a day of serious work. Her serene countenance was jarring; was *she* pulling away from *him*? He found himself drawn by the possibility that the decision was not his to make, then dismissed it.

He looked at her buttoned coat, the old black mittens she wore for serious winter walking, the water- and snow-stained fur-lined boots she reserved for weekends. His voice was playful. "This is not a city to walk in at midnight."

She looked at him, feeling like a child who had bundled up exactly as Mommy had insisted before braving the elements. A wise child. "No city is a city to walk in at midnight." She was wrapping a wool scarf around her neck.

"You'll get mugged." He was taking his time, sure of himself. She was pulling on a hat, an old stocking cap she'd saved from college days, with a pompon at the tip.

"You'll get attacked, raped." All said gently, singsong. He eyed her deliberately now that she'd finished stuffing herself into layers of clothing. "Well, maybe not raped." He smiled slowly, with affection. She smiled back, and turned to leave. "Honey. Talk to me." His voice was languid, self-assured. She thought she heard him patting the bed; she stopped at the door and turned around.

"I've got a knot inside. I just need to give it room to uncoil. A walk, that's all."

"Can't we talk about it? You'll feel better if you get it out."

She paused for a moment. "All right." She walked back to the bed and sat beside him. "It's Grace Healy. I can't get her out of my mind."

He stared at her. "Healy?"

His mouth was open as she rushed on. "You remember. The woman with all the kids, the one I did the series on at Christmas. All that money pouring in, all those gifts, used toys, old sweaters. Well, it isn't Christmas anymore, no one feels guilty anymore, and she's right back where she was. I feel so goddamn helpless. See? It doesn't help to talk about it." She kissed his unbelieving face, feeling as she had the first time she had made love on top, and left the apartment.

The cold sobered her the moment she hit the street, her cleverness, her gamesmanship a rank, moldering thing called into service over too many years. Saving face. Saving nothing. She made her way in the wind to Suzanne's, six blocks up, two across, approached only by a cabbie slowing at the curb, looking for a fare.

It was only when she got there that she remembered she'd have to press that dead-awakening buzzer to get in; probably scare the hell out of Suzanne. Two short bleeps. Please Suzie, don't swallow your heart, just answer.

She heard the sleepy incredulous voice inquiring through the speaker.

"It's me, I'm okay, just cold."

"Dope." The buzzer screeched horribly; she could still hear it when she was at the elevator. Suzanne always gave people extra time to fumble with the door.

She was waiting, wearing the usual lacy nightgown, ethereal, romantic, sexy, so incongruous with her scrubbed face, her matted hair lopsided from the pile of pillows she slept on.

"Love your hat," Suzanne said.

"I didn't wake the kids, did I?"

"Only a man can do that. They've had their antennae up for possible suitors, not to mention possible sex, for years." Suzanne helped her off with her layers. "You're wearing stuff you must have kept since college, I recognize some of it. I'll get the brandy."

Beth looked mildly surprised. "Is there a connection here that I'm missing?"

"Well, you've always wrapped yourself up in girlish clothes when you were scared or needed reassurance. And brandy has curative qualities when the wind is howling and your heart is beating like a bass drum—*et voilà,*" she said, as she found two glasses and poured. "Drink."

Beth took a sip, then tucked her feet up, curling her toes. "Substitute this with vanilla Cokes and we could be back in the dorm."

"With two babies who are nearly as tall as I am stashed in the bedrooms? A likely story. Besides, would you really want to go back?

"Yes. No."

"How quickly we've gone from anticipation to equivocation; I can remember when we knew everything!"

"Not everything," Beth said.

"Tell me something I didn't know."

"You didn't know I slept with Dennis Mayo. That's how I got pregnant; it was him, not Donald."

"I think I knew that," Suzanne said.

"You didn't. You absolutely didn't!"

"Well, yes and no. I knew it wasn't Donald. I knew that viscerally, I can't explain it, I just did. And I guess I didn't consciously know it was Dennis. But who else did we know who would have let that happen and then not own up to it?"

"Did Georgie know?"

"In line with the everything we all knew, she wouldn't have permitted such a thought to enter her head."

Suzanne watched her old friend with growing concern, which she tried not to convey. She sensed that it wasn't the fact of Dennis Mayo that was gnawing at Beth, although betrayal was hardly a comforting memory. There was something else, something more. She waited.

"I wish I could say that I never had a moment's peace, that my little secret burned inside me relentlessly, but that isn't true. I buried it very successfully; I made believe so well that eventually I convinced myself it never happened—not Dennis, not even the baby. And all the while I knew there was no risk, that Dennis would never say anything because it didn't *mean* anything to him. It went out of his head, just like all those girls in San Francisco did when he was married to Georgie. See how clever I was?"

"It wasn't an evil thing to do, to survive. You were a scared kid who wanted to get on with her life."

"But I did it so easily, so well. I never really suffered. It was as if I was exempt from the rules, above them somehow. Well, I was so beautiful, everyone said so. Boys were always falling all over themselves to get near me—was it my fault? Could anything be my fault? The beautiful just *are,* right? Until they're not."

Suzanne was looking at her curiously. Was that it? Was Beth afraid of losing her looks? Well, Suzanne knew how *that* felt, or perhaps what she knew more precisely was the fear of general disintegration, the sagging here, the cellulite there. She herself had never been beautiful. Oh, she was attractive enough, but it was the loss of youth she could relate to, not the erosion of great beauty. And she had to admit that she thought it would be far better to be old and exquisite—which she was certain Beth would be—rather than just old. Perhaps this was why she had imagined that Beth would be spared the helpless agitation aging often engendered among those most vulnerable: women.

And of course Beth knew better than to admit that she wasn't. As close as she was to Suzanne, she couldn't imagine how she could possibly tell her how frightened she had become by the realization that she was losing her beauty, slowly perhaps, but inevitably. Nor could she explain the curious phenomenon whereby once you took notice, once the signs caught your unwilling eye, the process seemed to escalate furiously, scaring the very life out of you as you watched. To anyone else this would, she knew, sound like a sickening plaint—poor thing, once young and beautiful, having to grow older like any ordinary mortal, lose your edge and find other ways to get by. But the edge was precisely the point; she'd done nothing to create it or deserve it, but had grown accustomed to it, even dependent upon it and the deference it bred. To be beautiful was to be set apart. It made no difference if one had nothing else to offer, or everything else; if one used it shamelessly or not at all. Knowing better changed nothing; Beth knew better than to assign it full value, to rely upon it as a central force, and still it became fundamental to her life. It was a matter of one's effect on others, in a society that placed so high a value on physical perfection as to cause young girls who thought they were ugly to want to die, and billion-dollar industries that promised a remedy, any remedy, to thrive.

"Do you worry about getting old?" Beth said, attempting a passing interest.

"Sometimes. In the middle of the night I think about dying, or maybe I dream about it. It used to paralyze me with fear to contemplate death even for a second, but lately I find the thought of it has a calming effect. Maybe because I can't really comprehend it. It's not like when we were kids and knew we were never going to die. Still, I can't seem to wind my mind around the finality of it, the blankness. So I think about Jack Kennedy and Cary Grant having gone through it and it makes me feel better. Getting older is something else entirely—you have to live with that."

"I worry about all of it, aging, dying, more often than I'm comfortable admitting," Beth said.

"I read the column; it was wonderful." And how in hell did I imagine it was for the rest of us, and not for you? "Maybe you're feeling this now because a false pregnancy brought back the past—the Beth you used to be. I think any life, upon examination, comes up short, at least to the one living it. But you're not that person anymore, the one who starred in those memories; you're not even the person you were yesterday."

"What's going to happen to us, do you think?" Beth asked, although she was quite certain she knew, at least where she was concerned, that only less and less of the same was in store.

"You'll go to Tuscany and write dark, sexual, Gothic novels. Georgie will buy a house that needs to be restored plank by plank, molding by molding, which she will do meticulously well. And I'll probably find the right man when I'm, oh, seventy-seven or so, and we'll go doddering off into the sunset."

"That doesn't sound so bad," Beth said, thinking, *at least you'll have your children.*

"Not bad at all," Suzanne said, thinking, *at least you'll have your looks.*

They sat silently for a while, comforted by each other's presence, and the brandy. Then Beth became agitated again.

"I can't believe I did that—just let Georgie go off with Dennis without saying a word, when I could have warned her about him, maybe saved her all that heartache when they were in San Francisco!"

"Do you really think anything you might have said could have stopped her? She was crazy about Dennis. And Georgie knew what we all knew then: that marriage was the key. The key to the door that would keep us safe for*ever.* It was why we were sent to college, in our high socks and plaid skirts. What did we dream about anyway, being physicists? Corporate executives? Look at us—you wrote, I painted, Georgie rebelled—do you notice we chose things you could do at home? The kinds of choices that would cause fathers to say to their sons, "Yes, but what are you going to do for a *living*?" We were stuck and we didn't know it. The ultimate statement Georgie could make was to marry Dennis; was there a barricade to storm? Not for Eisenhower babies. Listen, Beth, that girl who used to be you did a dumb thing years and years ago, got caught, found a way to solve it. It helped her become the sensitive, perceptive woman you are today. Put it behind you."

Walking home in a light rain, hearing only her own footsteps, Beth saw no evil lurking in the shadowed corners, imagined no sudden, swift waylay by menacing dark men. A southern girl after all, who believed in absolution. Only the future scared her to death.

nine

Georgie folded the newspaper so that only Beth's article was visible, as if to isolate the story she told from the real tragedies on the pages surrounding it. After all, Georgie had been prepared for this, forewarned by Beth, who had spilled every detail in a rush of delayed guilt—and had even asked Georgie's permission to write about it.

And Georgie had thought, *why not?* Beth favored story pieces that went at tough personal subjects, told through an unnamed character who was often someone she'd encountered or heard about, sometimes someone she knew well; sometimes even herself. The attitude, though, was always Beth's. She'd always bring it round to her own point, the point irrevocably tied to an issue which could be explosive or poignant or merely an undercurrent tugging at people's lives, unrecognized until now. Georgie had always thought that was the genius of Beth's work: the separation of heartbeats, a reining-in that allowed for the momentary illusion of wisdom and its comfort.

This article was no different; it was just that Georgie had never been a knowing subject before, and she found it unnerving. Here was her old friend writing about her—writing about the three of them, their proud triumvirate, as if they were specimens under glass: Fifties Girls. But why should it matter? Why should any of it matter, even the lie exposed; it was a million years ago!

Only yesterday.

Lew, directly across from her at the kitchen table, thought how young Georgie looked, engrossed, off her guard. They had made love the night before; it always showed in her face. But these days, no, these years, he had come to think of sex between them as an act of necessity, as purely functional, for Georgie like the filling of a gas tank. Still agile despite the burden of her strained flesh, her breasts engorged as if from milk, she had only to arch her back and offer that satin sweetness for him to suck and he would feel the heat in him, that mindless heat betraying the child in the man, and when her nipples were on fire she would spread her legs, tearing his mouth away, pulling him up and into her, and he would lunge again and again, his face over hers, willing her to look at him, to see him. She didn't then. He couldn't remember if she ever had. It was entirely possible that all through his married life he had made love alone.

He supposed he should be grateful for her desire, and hated himself immediately for the reflexive nature of the thought, for its bending quality; then he wondered what he expected after more than twenty years of marriage, and forgave himself. Still, there were times when he wanted to kill her. He watched her reading what was undoubtedly Beth's article—what other parts of the paper did Georgie bother to read? She seemed to cull her opinions from her friend, whose interests were broad enough to give Georgie a sentence or two on nearly anything people were liable to speak of these days.

He had been stunned by Beth when he first saw her, felt the beginnings of an erection at his own wedding from the sight of pale blue silk wrapped around the body of his wife's best friend. But then the bride herself was so lovely, so beyond his expectations, he'd recovered quickly, easily. *This* woman was attainable.

He had spent the first several years of his marriage wondering how that could be so, how Lew Gregory could possibly have pulled that off. Waiting to be found out, waiting for the error to be caught. Years later, in bed with a secretary whose carnal knowledge was legendary although purely imaginative for those who informed of it, Lew found himself inexplicably chosen once again. This time he adapted with ease, and spent four months regarding his cock as a newly purchased ornament symbolizing success.

He had wandered into a fog, that was all. And wandered out again, wincing at the shallowness, the predictability of his swan song. Lorrie. Lor*een.* She had never heard of Adlai Stevenson; that was a girl's name, wasn't it? He couldn't get an erection that night. Lord knows she tried, but he couldn't. And that was the beginning of the end. With Georgie, the end was at the beginning—that was it, wasn't it? The moment you buy a car its value diminishes, the moment you love a woman you get handouts on a whim, like pigeons in the park. You are watched, curiously, as you partake, odd creature that you are. Feed elsewhere and you will suffer the wrath of your sometime benefactor, the one who had got there first. But he hadn't, he hadn't! He had come home to an all too understanding, easily forgiving wife, and that had hurt worst of all. What did he want then, emotional chaos, wild recriminations, slammed doors, sleepless nights? Feel, Georgie, feel!

"You're red," Georgie said.

"What?"

"You're all red. Your face. Are you all right?"

"Fine. I'm fine."

"How many miles did you run?"

She was holding him there, wanting to talk. He would make a joke. He would say, was it good for you? Did the earth move?

"Three," he said.

She held him still longer, asking him to cut down and run every other day during the winter. Careful not to suggest that age was a factor, that she worried about his heart, she pointed out there was a flu going around. This he took in with responsible nods and some perplexity. He heard the plea in her voice and recognized it as guilt, but for what?

As he left to catch his train it occurred to him that on those rare occasions when they had sex, she too became disjointed, as if a vague memory hung between them. He perceived this as a mirror with dual images, the one facing out for his eyes only, his desperate eyes, showed a puzzle of infinite complexity which he could not grasp; the other, facing inward, on which Georgie's eyes were always fixed, kept her safe. She didn't sound safe this morning. Perhaps, without even realizing it, he had reached her after all. He had reached Loreen, hadn't he? A mere wading pool, but he'd whipped it into shuddering foam. And the vast sea that was his wife was not serene this morning.

The train was pulling into the station as he arrived. He ran for it, feeling invincible.

Georgie read the article yet again. It was a backward glimpse of the end of an era, the 1950s, by way of a story about friendship and an episode of deceit among three college girls. The point, ostensibly, was to illuminate the extraordinary sociological changes that had occurred since then, particularly with regard to women and the honesty between them. The protagonist had gotten into trouble (the old euphemism for pregnant) at the age of nineteen, light-years before teenage pregnancy—not to mention teenage sex—would become commonplace. And trouble was the right word: abortion was illegal, expensive, unsafe . . . nor could she turn to her boyfriend, with whom she was a "good" girl who did not go "all the way." The boy responsible, the one with whom her repressed sexuality had exploded, belonged to someone else; one of the girls, in fact, in this tight threesome. Still she turned to them for help, and of course they came through, stood by her, protected her, cleaned up after her. Never knowing how low she had sunk, or the depth of her gratitude. Yet as the years went by, memory receded and paled until she was almost convinced none of it had happened. But one never really gets off; justice comes around and extracts payment, as every fifties girl should know. And so she had not been allowed to disremember forever. Now she saw she had had other choices back then, even in that world of nasty female webs, woven out of boredom and frustration. Today, she hoped, she treasured her women friends enough to risk their judgment and trust their forgiveness.

Georgie took her coffee and walked around her house, through the dining room and the study and the living room, eying furniture, rugs, wallpaper and fixtures, with her mouth slack, her mind dulled. She could not remember choosing half the things that were there, but she knew she had. She could not remember the vision in her mind that caused her to act with such surety, opting for this, dismissing that. It had all been so specific, so definitive, the way she had set about turning this vast home into a statement. Looking at it now, she had no idea what it said. What she had once needed it to say. There was silence now, yet she felt no terror. This mélange of things, of ornaments, was merely bewildering.

She dressed with special care, laying out each article neatly, savoring its touch as she gingerly stepped into it and pulled it to her; making the time go, willing it, as women will when they have nothing left to do. Still, only a few moments passed. She worked on her hair, and it fell immediately, miraculously, into place. Her makeup took longer, but not enough. A whole day was left.

Well, of course, she had a million things to do.

She had to go to the market, and the cleaners, and there was an antique show she'd promised she'd go to with Sally. But Sally, a neighborhood friend, would fill her in on the latest verbal violence that passed for communication in her marriage, wallowing in her woes; a little scorn, a little disdain would make her wail palatable, but Sally hadn't a sardonic bone in her body. Georgie thought to spare herself, but for what? She'd find something.

At the market she found herself wondering how many times she had shopped for food in her life, how many times she had fingered tomatoes, dug in for string beans, pressed melons, stared at rows of meat until somehow divining what to make for dinner for a family of this size, then this size, until finally there was just the two of them again, she and Lew. She remembered how in the beginning, as a newlywed, the supermarket had seemed like a vast maze; how she'd clutch her list in her hand as she pushed the cart around, surprises awaiting at every turn—what fun! What fun stocking the shelves, the pantry, like a real grown-up in a real house. Then the babies came—how marvelous being a real woman, with a womanly purpose! More to buy, more to stock, more to cook, more to feed, oh my.

But it wasn't the daily trivia that told the story; one had to step back to view accomplishments, assess conditions, rationalize failures, measure, rate, judge; be found wanting.

She thought of Suzanne, who had wanted to paint since she had known her but could never quite raise herself to the risk, certainly not publicly. Yet she belittled what she *had* done, when to Georgie the creation of commercials was altogether fascinating and mysterious. She had often tried to imagine what Suzanne and Dale actually did each day, and how they actually did it; she would walk past buildings on Third and Lexington avenues in Manhattan and wonder about the worlds inside them, sometimes seeing young women, girls really, pushing through the doors with alacrity, and feeling alarmed at her own ignorance, her inexperience in this new age of opportunity.

She knew what Beth did. Beth who back then had made them swear not to go to Donald and kill him or say one word. And of course they hadn't, her good friends, her best friends. Later, when he married her, they forgave him. Sort of. Poor innocent Donald, who, she now knew, had done nothing.

At the cleaners Georgie was thinking of San Francisco; of how she and Suzanne had exchanged thick letters regularly, yet she had never heard from Beth, not once. But when Georgie came home Beth seemed so happy to have her back. Now she knew it was simply Beth's relief that Georgie's blindness to her affair with Dennis was still intact.

But how frightened she must have been of Georgie's reproof, of her indignation. And for what, for Dennis? A night with Dennis? Half the girls in San Francisco had spent a night with Dennis!

It seemed they had both monumentally misjudged his importance, his worth. For Georgie, though, the consequences were far greater: with the grim determination of a girl who believes that heartbreak has turned her into a woman, she strode into a passionless marriage—in permanent, private mourning for her one great love.

Dennis. Graceless reprobate, whose lust knew no bounds. How had she permitted so unworthy a memory to become her life's frame of reference? The "all" to the years' "nothing"?

She drove to the antique show alone, pointing her car there merely to masquerade as a woman of purpose, yet with only a faint hope of diversion. It was a crowded hall, an old armory that remained austere even with treasures on display. She saw a Queen Anne desk and wondered if a woman had ever sat there and written her foolish heart out, and knew at once a woman had; women had. She saw occasional tables and settees and hand-painted cabinets, all at outrageous prices, prices she had once paid to create a setting for the person she had decided to be. In such ways does money permit delusion. Her mother had known this and had been grateful for it.

Why should she be allowed to have money? Ah, why should Beth be allowed to have beauty? She was reminded of a game the three of them had invented at school. Called "Justice," it was born out of some long-forgotten slight as an attempt to bring the wounded among them from tears to laughter, based as it was on sweet revenge. And so, the professor who adamantly refused to believe that Beth had left her English Lit paper on the plane back from Washington would deliver his next lecture before two hundred students with his fly open; Georgie's father, having responded with astounding prejudice and stupidity when his daughter suggested he resign from his exclusively white Protestant country club, would pass his next life as a black Hasidic Jew in Mississippi; and Donald, having gotten Beth pregnant and gotten off scot-free, would spend eternity trying to reason with terrible twos. None of this happened.

On the way home, steeped in thought, Georgie took a wrong turn. She found herself in a town just a few miles from her own, one in which she'd never been. She drove the streets slowly in this familiar foreign land, without curiosity or panic at her lost bearings, her instincts setting her right despite a lack of desire.

It occurred to her that if there really was any justice, she would be allowed to disappear here, effortlessly, swallowed by a mist.

ten

On the shuttle flight back from Washington, Beth tried to remember why it had seemed so imperative to veer off and see her mother, after an exhaustive day of gathering information for a column. What had she expected, beyond the usual disapproval, of that frail woman who still moved as if to receive the beneficence due her as her daddy the senator's girl?

Her grandfather's photos still dominated the piano; Beth had to strain to find the one picture of her father, taken on the beach at Rehobeth in '46, with his children clinging to him—their warrior come home, finally safe. The wind had caught them when her mother took that shot, that every-family beach scene of innocent exuberance. It was not until years later that Beth recognized the look of bewilderment on her father's face. Had it been the war, his astonishment at being alive? Her mother's drinking? She'd never know.

Her brothers had married, borne children, and remained in the south; Washington *was* the south for those who hadn't poured in from Ohio and California, Nebraska and New York to churn reward from the sleepy capital, imprinting their various rhythms, tones, desires. Such Yankees settled in Bethesda, Chevy Chase and Potomac, in Fairfax and Alexandria and Reston, and lived right alongside real Marylanders and Virginians in these bedroom communities of the seat of power.

Beth's family house on Creek Road was freshly painted, looking hopeful, like an old girl who believed her makeup could turn the clock back. Her mother was in the "sun-room," a porch that had been closed in years before with walls of glass, where plants thrived and people shivered. She was with her ladies, or what remained of the group Beth had long ago given up trying to sort out.

Delilah she knew and spotted immediately, grateful that death hadn't carried her off. Delilah was a big woman, towering over the others, such fragile, sunken shells; her voice boomed over their murmurs like a call to life. She had been awkward in her youth, but, buoyed by a trust fund, Delilah had blossomed into a belle of her own sort, casting off husbands with the neat regret of her friends snipping off dead buds. She had married four times and was now a widow, having finally gotten it right, she would say, laughing. Delilah looked far younger than her years, fat smoothing out her wrinkles, shoring up her slackening cheeks.

Beth's mother had greeted her with raised eyebrows.

"Well," she said, the word leaving a trail of land mines strewn with daisies.

She bent to kiss her mother, who raised her cheek as someone hissed, "Who's that?" and another whispered, much too loudly, "That's Elizabeth Ann from New Yauk."

"Bethie, you come over here and let me see you!" Delilah roared from the far end of the room, where she was presiding over a hot game of rummy. Smiling broadly, she pronounced Beth as pretty as ever, and swooped her up into her arms.

Later, sitting with her tea, Beth peered sidelong into her mother's cup and wondered if its contents was laced with whiskey. She didn't begrudge her that, not now: when people are close to death we permit them their idiosyncrasies; we tend to wink at actions that might once have wreaked havoc. Her mother's excessive drinking hadn't exactly done that, she'd hidden it well; hidden everything well.

Having taken Beth through the usual quiz, the ladies, her mother included, went on about their business: they sipped, nibbled cakes, and challenged one another's remembrances. Sometimes Beth was asked to be the arbiter; mostly, they seemed to forget she was there.

Her mother rose abruptly to go to the kitchen, her walk more springlike and determined than Beth would have thought possible, the walk of a young woman needing to get away, needing relief, finding it exactly where she'd hidden it. Her brothers hadn't known about their mother's drinking, though they were older; Beth had, but only because at sixteen she had once been where she wasn't expected, and stumbled upon the result. How she'd agonized, how she'd needed desperately to know why, why. Her father had died with the secret, or with his own perplexity. Or maybe he had known as one knows when a love affair has made its first subtle shift, that chill for which there are no words. Did he blame himself for her drinking? Was it the children who tipped her over, scrubbed to perfection for company, squeezing out her everyday life? Beth and her brothers had instinctively tiptoed through childhood in their own house, saving their exuberance for the world at large, which paid them little mind. It seemed to her now that they sensed their mother had been staggered by the full realization of her lot in life, although she'd been groomed for nothing else.

Beth went after her mother now, and found her with a bottle in her hand poised over her cup. She stopped in midair only for an instant of calm acknowledgment. And then continued pouring. She placed another cup on the table, filled it with tea and motioned Beth to sit.

"You surprised me, dropping in like this."

Chastised, although she hadn't any idea what her latest infraction might have been, embarrassed at her childlike acquiescence, Beth wished she still smoked so she could light up and feel like a grown-up.

"Well, since your father died what reason would you have?" her mother continued easily.

"Mother." For she had come home since then, of course she had, Christmas, one Easter, a Thanksgiving. Ah. Holidays, generated by propriety.

"There's no point in being old if you can't say what you think. You were always your father's girl." She said this firmly, looking pleased with herself, as if it had taken great determination to finally spill it when in fact she'd been saying it for years. But Beth couldn't rise up for it, not now. A look of expectation arched her mother's features for a moment, then slid away.

"We really are up there in years, you know," she said, chirpy in the face of doom. "We all just sit around chattering away about nothing, the dead, the past. Sulie's half senile, May Catherine is dying." She shrugged. "Don't look so pained. It's all right, really. It's over, that's all. But there are still the days. We fill each other's silences. No one else, well, speaks our language I guess you would say."

"Delilah?"

"She's as healthy as a horse." Beth's mother laughed. "Are you still seeing that fellow, uh . . ."

"Robert."

"Yes. Robert." She said the name carefully, as one would a new word. "Are you?"

Yes and no flew through Beth's mind. "Yes."

"You haven't come to me about *ro*-mance," she said.

"No," Beth said, suddenly wishing she had, wishing she could. Her mother, unperturbed, took a healthy swallow from her cup.

"Remember when I broke the Chinese vase?"

Her mother nodded with interest, remembering Beth's confusion when the pieces of the vase were finally discovered; having hidden them, she eventually convinced herself that the accident had never occurred, thus she would not have to answer for it and needn't make herself ill with worry, as children sometimes do when they know they will cause an uproar. And she did cause one.

"Have you been hiding something again?" her mother asked, suddenly looking young, eager.

"It was all so long ago. I should have told you then, but I just didn't have the courage, I thought it would be the end of the world. Even now, I'm afraid I may shock you, hurt you. I don't mean to; it just seems terribly important to undo the lies, and try to let it go." She heard herself rushing and strained for an easy pace, as if it would temper this irretrievable error in her life. Her mother's face had sagged, but her chin remained high.

"I don't know how to say this," Beth said, shaking her head hopelessly. She took a deep breath. "My senior year, when you thought I took a semester in Paris? Well, I didn't. I wasn't in

France. I was in Pennsylvania, in a place where . . . in a home for unwed mothers. I was pregnant." She stole a look at her mother, who sat motionless, only her eyes popping in alarm. "I gave the child up for adoption. A little girl."

A moment of silence went by, perhaps two. Both women gave it their attention.

Beth sighed involuntarily. Her mother turned to face her.

"Why do you tell me this? Why now?" she said, her heart still thumping in her throat.

Beth held her gaze. "I'll never have children, it's too late for that now. But I did have this one child—even though that's all I did, have her—even though she was never really mine. I thought you had a right to know that she existed, someone related to us."

Her mother made as if to sip her tea, then placed the cup down very carefully. "I already have grandchildren." Then, as if suddenly hearing what her daughter heard, she tried to rouse herself. "I'm sorry," she said, stabbing awkwardly at compassion. "It must have been terrible for you."

Beth looked at her mother's passive face, regained by a lifelong devotion to composure. She felt as if she was in a confessional where the priest had nodded off while she was admitting to murder.

"Sometimes I think I'm disappearing," Beth ventured. "I look in the mirror and see someone else entirely. And somehow all the old reflexes, the habits of thought, the little mind twists that carried me through so neatly, no longer apply. I have to get some new ones for this stranger I've become, but I don't know where."

Her mother was looking at her intently now, but Beth didn't notice; she was staring into space, sure she'd lost her audience.

"It isn't working with Robert," Beth went on. "It's drifting away, I know it. I even know what to do about it; I've been in this situation so many times before, with so many other men. I'd begun to think the men were interchangeable, but it isn't them, not really. It's me, I'm the one who's played the same part too many times before, I'm the one who isn't convincing anymore. I keep thinking there's another way to do this, another way to be, another person I could become, but she eludes me. I see other women my age who have a look of tranquility, a kind of grace that emanates from within. I envy them, and I feel a terrible failure. I seem to have missed the point, or lost it. How did I do that? How did it happen?" Suddenly aware of her surroundings, Beth was astonished that she'd said such things in her mother's presence, not yet realizing she was spilling exactly what she had come to tell, hoping for enlightenment, begging for love. Knowing better. This was the daughter she was, this was the mother she had.

"You're really such a child, Elizabeth," her mother said, recovering.

Beth the daughter was immediately on her guard.

"You got what you wanted, and now you don't want it anymore. Well, you didn't want to be like us, did you?" she said, sweeping her arm towards the ladies in the sun-room. "You wanted to be free of all that, you wanted to have a career, and *men*—not a husband and children."

"I married Donald," Beth said, drawn automatically to her own defense.

"A childless marriage that ended in divorce," her mother said, dismissing ten years with ease. She sat taller in her chair, righteousness propelling her. "The world once made sense, you know. There was balance and order when we were coming up, there was duty, selflessness. But now women expect to have their cake and eat it too. They want love and marriage and children, but only if they can have them with no responsibility, so they can tend to their *real* work. It's amazing, absolutely amazing, and instead of a better world we've got broken homes and aimless children and," she said pointedly, gathering breath, "middle-aged career women who thought they knew everything and have suddenly discovered they missed something. Only they can't get it back. It's too late."

Her mother shrugged and bit into a cookie, her reward for having engaged in this bout of motherhood with her aging child. What she had really wanted to say was, Why can't I know some of the affection, some of the love you showered on your father? For it seemed she never had. But her daughter would have countered, Why can't you talk to me like a mother, like someone who loves me, who truly cares? For it seemed she never did. And so their meeting ground always had to be forged anew, a place of mutual dissatisfaction, mutual regret.

"You know," her mother said, suddenly remembering, "when Tally Munson went to Paris and wanted to treat you to something better than a student meal, you were nowhere to be found. That silly little French girl concocted one story after another for three weeks. Tally was never terribly bright, poor thing, but I knew something was up. I kept expecting to get a wire announcing that you'd eloped with Donald."

"And when you didn't, weren't you concerned?" Beth asked. "Or at least curious?"

Her mother straightened up. "You were always an independent child, Elizabeth. When I wanted you to wear your hair off your face, you cut bangs."

It was Delilah who hugged her before she left; Delilah who

said, "I'm so proud of you, honey, I still get goose bumps every time I see your name in the paper." Delilah to whom she would respond, with gratitude, for the soothing, blind belief characteristic of mothers.

On the way back to New York it seemed to Beth that it was her mother who had gotten what she wanted and then didn't want it anymore: she'd had a home, husband, children, all that was expected, yet she'd suffered an awful malaise and turned it into wretched excess, becoming an alcoholic. Then as times changed she heaped scorn on the choices suddenly available for women, choices that she herself had never had, that might have saved her. Or might not. Such things were never neat. But, contrary to her mother's pronouncement, Beth had gotten what she wanted and still wanted it, at least where wanting could be contained and measured: she had her work. Her work was her anchor, her connection, her use. It depended only upon what she produced, and would take her through the remaining decades of her life. It was a matter of value, of inner confirmation, of constructive purpose.

In her writing, she knew, she limited herself to a narrow field, conscious of the relative safety of its parameters, of the need to confine that to which she dared aspire. She was not a journalist in the pure sense of the word, nor a feature writer: rather she was an observer who chose whatever news or trend she wished, and reflected upon its ordinary effect—the excesses of power, the gender gap, drunk driving, AIDS, arms control, child abuse, capital punishment, Manhattan's homeless, Ireland's children, *Glasnost,* greed. She brought it all home, personalized it, and thus found its center, and was told she did this well. She half believed it. Her other half knew there were times when she cheated, reached into her bag of writer's tricks to haul herself out of a bind and was admired anyway. Having developed a certain reputation, she was read positively: readers approached her work with value already assigned, allowing her lesser efforts to escape scrutiny.

Robert's praise, then, with its lack of shading, had always been disquieting—did he love her too much to be discerning about her work, or did he love her too little? She knew it was the very fact that she was published that sealed her worth in his eyes. She had experienced that herself, in the beginning—an article on foolscap seemed to have *how dare you presume* stamped all over it, only to be legitimized by its appearance in print. She knew better now. She knew too much, that was it. Knew her own limitations, and Robert's: could not help but see that in his eyes her success legitimized *him.* And he had loved her for it.

Then why did she want to hold on to him, when she didn't want to be anyone's streak of light, having to sit in the dark there by herself? She was weary. Weary of starting over, and over, and over, one man after another. Talking herself into and out of countless scenes, dramas, beginnings, endings, confined to that limbo where one may or may not get there from here, soaring one moment, grasping at ledges the next. Was there serenity in a slower death? She didn't know, anymore than she knew how it was that a woman who had toughed it out in the grimy sexist bullpen of the newspaper where she'd started, had forged friendships, generated grudging respect, and with a fierce tenacity, a will, broke through the ranks of her peers to that rarefied place, read now in soon-to-be three hundred markets, how it was that such a woman was always done in, in the end, by the basic nature of her sex: her want of a man.

Not any man, of course. Probably not Robert. This was a

good thing, because when she arrived home it soon became clear that he was gone. His clothes were emptied from the closets, the medicine cabinet's old, rusted shelves were suddenly and unappealingly naked on the right side.

His note, filled with regret, said he would call. She hoped not. He had merely done what she hadn't the courage or the stamina to do. He had found the courage and the stamina with another woman; Beth knew this instinctively and was curiously unmoved.

eleven

For weeks Suzanne and Neal had been living together, out in the open; Neal had finally separated from his wife. They were giddy with happiness, the children erupting at every expression of this unexpected windfall, this bounty: Neal. Neal living in their house, with their mother, with them, every day. Suzanne knew it was too good and embraced it anyway. How could she help it?

Then something happened. But just as she couldn't isolate the moment when she had given in to Neal, allowed herself to slide into his insistence and be overtaken, she could not find the error, the snag; could only feel the unraveling.

It was she who reacted to the cold, the heat, she whose sensors were at the edge of her skin, she who feared loss. And while she supposed it was always so, among couples—that one cut the path while the other tried to find a foothold—she no more understood how she had become so bare, so vulnerable with Neal than how it had always been so with men, all of her life.

They returned from a movie, where she had sat like a stone, because he had. Now they sat on the couch, disconnected; she was trying to breathe, as fear, the only fear she had ever known with him that wasn't eased within minutes, seconds, threatened to squeeze the life from her. He rubbed his face and said he was tired; it came out like a heavy sigh, a sufferer's due. She suggested they go up to bed, sleep on her mind, not sex, thinking of course that if she didn't ask he wouldn't tell and it wouldn't be so, whatever it was . . . evade the doctor, stay healthy. Neal had gotten his diagnosis elsewhere, which hit Suzanne like a flash when he spoke.

"I'm depressed," he said. "I don't know what's wrong. I love you, but I can't . . ." The words hung there like a fat balloon; can't what? can't what? "I know this is crazy, I don't expect you to understand when I don't understand it myself."

He'd been seeing his wife; that she understood. In the last few weeks there had been odd nights when he worked unusually late. Suzanne had chosen to think nothing of it but perhaps she had chosen ignorance; had his wife chosen it before her?

"Suzanne, I love you, I've always loved you, there's never been any question about that, there never will be." She loved his oaths, so sweeping and insistent. But his face, normally deflective of time and the elements, looked cruelly lined, ashen, his shoulders hunched from the weight of inflicting pain righteously. "I have to go back to Lynn," he said, meaning the wife from whom he'd separated.

Neal looked at Suzanne's horribly stricken face, that betrayer of her most wretched self. He took her hand and kissed it gently, never taking his eyes from hers. "Just for a short time," he said. "Not forever. We're talking about weeks, that's all. I promised her I'd give it one more try. It won't work, it never has, but if I do this . . . oh God, don't cry, you and Daniel and Annie are my family, my life. Just let me do this, and then we'll have the rest of our lives."

This was a very careful man, she knew. Once in her presence he had failed to defend a friend and colleague who was being maliciously maligned because, he explained, it wouldn't have been politic to do so. Suzanne had strongly protested his inaction. It was the only time she could remember transcending her feelings for him, viewing him without the imprimatur of a thoroughly besotted lover. Now he was explaining again. He was asking her permission to play out a charade, to go back to Lynn with, ostensibly, every good intention, believing all the while there was no chance for success, thus causing it to be so. His purpose, Suzanne knew, was to appear to have gone the extra mile, so as to be absolved of any blame for the marriage having failed. It was, at best, a peculiar route to impunity, yet very much identifiable with Neal. That this occurred to her at all, most particularly at a moment of emotional chaos, surprised Suzanne. By now her tears had crusted on her cheeks; a few ran down her collar.

She had no idea how long they sat there, Neal murmuring words of love, promises of their future, Suzanne so physically weary she felt as if pinned to the spot by some huge, relentless object. Still her mind beckoned: that there was little ahead but more anguish was indisputable; that her facility for romanticizing, her hunger for more than love, for ardent belief, had gotten her into this quicksand, floated through her consciousness; it was more than she could yet take in.

When Neal finally rose to leave, she felt a sudden chill, as one does on awakening from a nap, as if Neal had been her own arms pressed against her, her own legs curled up, generating heat. At the door, they clung to each other like rag dolls; Neal whispered it would all be over soon. "Soon," he said yet again, wanting her affirmation, her faith. She could dredge up nothing, and closed the door.

She went back to the couch and sat in the mold shaped by the heaviness of her sorrow. Tears came anew, what endless well was this? But she'd had her first whiff of death and could not shake its scent: this was what it would be like without him. Why had she never thought about it, considered it, what had caused her to imagine she was exempt? The arrogance of love. When it is gone, one suffers cleanly; what is degrading is holding on. Suzanne knew this and still couldn't stop; she was careening at full tilt, fired by irrational hopes, drunk with the desire for love.

And so she prepared herself to wait the weeks. Zombie with a pasty smile, spy under cover, she told herself she'd pull it off. Neal would be back, and they'd resume their lives, with no one, especially the children, the wiser. At a restaurant that Tuesday with a client, she reached for her fork and imagined a scene from a film where the American posing as a German gives himself away by holding his fork in his right hand, and she froze. By Thursday Annie was seriously asking after Neal, and gave Suzanne a curious look when she prattled away about a business trip. It was only when she heard the echo of her own voice, its high-pitched trill, that she realized why she had aroused suspicion. Saturday night Daniel, newly won over by Neal, learned sarcasm: "Still away on business?" By the following week her children were mopey. The week after that they approached her with care, considerate of the invalid, uneasy in the face of her malady. Suzanne felt the screams inside her and clove to her silence. While she still had the presence of mind to feel uneasy at her complicity with the children, who after all had a stake in this too, her thoughts were almost entirely those of the desperate: convoluted, superstitious. She told herself that if she discussed the problem she would only lend it credence, and why upset the children if all was going to be well, soon enough? That they were already upset escaped her only because she could bear no more than the weight of her own leaden hopes.

Neal called every day and most nights, through the second week, and the third. And then a month had gone by. He began to come to the house again, as he had before his separation, at odd times when he wouldn't be missed. It was different now; he had to be home at an early hour, had to put in his time.

When he first appeared, Annie, overjoyed, rushed to him for her hugs; Daniel looked pleased in spite of himself, but hung back, wary again. Neal worked at it, too hard, and soon Daniel would have none of it and even Annie closed herself in her room; if sought out, she would respond, but only then; Daniel would not be moved. Neal seemed to have grown an alien cover, it clung to him like an overly sweet scent that put them all off. Suzanne thought it was his other identity, his other life.

She painted. Evenings, weekends, she removed herself from any consciousness of Neal—even, without intent or awareness, from her children—by immersing herself in her work. Where once she had created a lovable art, tenderly touched in, there was now a vitality, an almost ecstatic freedom. It was as if clarity was pulsing through her fingers while still eluding her grasp; as if, on canvas, she'd broken through her addiction to melodrama and its messianic highs and lows, as if she'd finally recognized this setup of her own making and balked, with a roar.

And she had never worked so well; she knew it. When Dale saw her output, he was instantly aware of her emergence to a new place beyond the strictures that he had always felt were self-imposed. But if fear, as Dale postulated, was the vise that contained her talent, how was it that now, in its sudden and terrible specificity, fear was fueling her? She didn't dwell on it, knew enough not to attempt to diagram the elusive links on this tenuous chain.

She had her lucid moments. Once, when Neal's wife was out of town, they had made love and fallen asleep curved around each other; when Suzanne awakened suddenly, hours before morning, she found him gone. She called him and raged at his insensitivity and he was contrite; he'd done it because of the neighbors, who were in on his marital stress, his role, his posture—what if they'd seen the *Times* lingering on his doormat when he always lunged for it at an early hour? What if they told Lynn, for they were *her* confidantes, that the moment she was gone he was out for the night? She dropped the phone in its cradle as if it were diseased, pulled her knees up to her chin and hugged them fiercely to stop her trembling.

It was true that she went about the usual business of covering it over, as she would a cigarette in the sand, but she was running out of smooth places where she could lay herself down. Lynn itched at her; the air, once so achingly fresh, was sour. All of her energies were required to keep her eye on the still-elusive future that rose like a glittering arch in a childlike mind, nor could she sweat or wheeze from the strain in his presence. Neal responded poorly when she displayed anything other than the composed, secure façade he had come to expect. He gave terse answers to her questions; hadn't they gone over this before? He tolerated her frustration; wasn't it hard for him, too? He acknowledged her pain; wouldn't they have the rest of their lives to assuage it? And when, in disgust with herself for having brought the subject up yet again, she apologized for this lapse in her serenity, he would dress her down gently for assuming the fault. And tell her she was wonderful.

She was playacting, of course. She had taken the part of Neal's Suzanne, her old self, and so it was the actress who was understanding, the actress who was patient and wise. It seemed as if Neal had written the script long ago, had fashioned her character by virtue of his view of her, which she now had to struggle, every day, to re-create. Yet who would she be if she wiped off the mask, scrubbed at it, tore at it; who was there?

Dale, having watched this unfold firsthand, was overtaken by feelings of enmity, at Neal, at his own helplessness, at the hoary consequences of love; perhaps most of all at Suzanne herself. While she could still manage to blunt Beth and Georgie's growing concern, she was stuck in Dale's presence day in and day out, and he gave her no room to equivocate. He presumed on their intimacy, using it as a bludgeon to whack at her fingers, to set her loose from disaster. Still she clung to it. "He's a fuck-up," Dale told her, "an emotional truant, and look what he's done to you. He throws you those expedient imponderables like doggy bones and you wag your little tail and he pats you. Christ!" She wasn't unmoved, she took his truth and stirred it into the well that fed her, propelled her, until it was no longer recognizable: lived with it.

In this way she kept her own counsel, preserving the essential vision with only her own distilled demons to keep in check. When they rose, and they did in times of panic, she beat them down mindlessly, as a wartime paratrooper exhorted to jump who could not afford to dwell on every macabre possibility.

She strained for the larger picture, the greater good, and did not even know that its base was being eroded in that small pocket within, where the eye is not blind. If she had, she'd have been grateful.

She was still sane.

twelve

Georgie loved her daughters deeply, but she adored her son Shawn. It was his mystery that held her; mystery always held. He had called this morning asking for money, his new-found freedom as a college freshman not at all diminished by the need to beg cash. Shawn sounded sweet even in his abruptness; he had never been much for telephones, always having one foot out the door. He had gone through a period of embarrassment at his mother's love, when he'd shut her out with a vengeance. Then he eased back to her, halfway, holding some new part of himself in a tight adolescent knot. The knot was loosening; Georgie took this as a sign that augured well for his future as a man.

She had called Melissa, her junior at Carlisle, the night before. Melissa was now living in the same dorm where Georgie, Beth and Suzanne had left their shadows a lifetime ago. But now there were men in the dorm, living side-by-side with the women, brushing their teeth with them, sharing bathrooms and who knew what-all, just like grown-ups in real life. Missy, who did not deserve her nickname (much to Georgie's relief) was in love with a senior named Tom Golden, a tall Jewish boy with a nice angular face, who had grown up in New Orleans and had never tasted a bagel until he got to Carlisle.

They were sleeping together; Georgie had known it instantly, from the way her softly chunky, fair-skinned child carried her body, the newfound grace. That had been in Melissa's freshman year, and it was only then that Georgie knew with certainty that her daughter had been a virgin up until that point. It was late in the game to feel sanguine, but Georgie did feel enormously grateful that her fear of an unwanted pregnancy, herpes, AIDS and an altogether ruined life, not to mention some groping adolescent male blundering through his first experience and ruining sex forever for her daughter, did not prompt her to hurl accusations at Melissa.

She dialed the brokerage firm in San Francisco where her oldest daughter Laura worked, and smiled instantly at the sound of the voice that answered. "Laura Gregory," it said, brisk, professional, confident.

"Miss Gregory, this is your mommy," Georgie said, enjoying herself.

"Hi, Mom, you called just in time, I just got in."

"How are you, honey?"

"Fine, terrific! They gave me a list, can you believe it? My very own customers! Small ones, you know, but mine. I was going to call you tonight and tell you. How's Dad?

"Fine. He's fine."

"What time is it there? Eleven-thirty? What are you doing home, you're usually off and running by now," Laura said.

"They gave you a list? That's fantastic!" Georgie said, wondering "off and running" where?

"I know, and I'm excited, but I'm scared too."

"That's good," Georgie said.

"Good! What's good about being afraid?"

"Honey, a little fear is healthy, it can propel you, give you that extra edge," Georgie said, suddenly aware of her inexperience in Laura's world, dispensing free advice worth every penny.

"But it's not a little fear, it's a whole big chunk. And it's dumb. I look at all these brokers as if they possess some kind of magic but I know they don't. Mom, I really think I can do it. I think I have a feel for it, a sense of it. There are times when I think I'll fly right by half the people here!"

Georgie listened to her daughter neatly dispose of her "fear" and was not at all concerned with Laura's ability to assess the situation. This was her clear-eyed, practical child; her grown-up. They talked for a few more moments, said words of love and then said good-bye. Afterwards, for a long while, Georgie sat by the phone thinking of nothing, wanting nothing, her eyes hooded.

Abruptly she got up and began cleaning the kitchen, not that it needed it; she needed to do it, needed the familiar motion. *This is me, I do this, I am here,* her hand pushing the sponge said.

She went at the kitchen floor, feeling her breasts sway as she mopped, and suddenly giggled . . . here was Georgie, known for cleaning up before the maid came, cleaning up now before baring the mess of her life: appearances counted, even in death. Poor Bud McFarlane! She'd heard about his suicide attempt and wept for him. Didn't the sonofabitch know you couldn't kill yourself with Valium? Sitting there in his cordovans, hell no, probably his Docksiders, the Lacoste shirt, chinos, that prep-school face, popping middle-class candy. And now he'd have to go back and face it, all of it, there are some people they just don't let die. Georgie wondered if she was one of them.

The problem was, she had gone as far as she could go. She was at an impasse, stuck. Is that how you felt, Bud? Judy? Marilyn? Julio Martinez, who jumped off the East River Bridge?

Here's how it was: I got carried away by my foolish heart's desire. And then, when it fell apart, I scrambled for the high ground, where no one can touch you—certain I had overstepped my limitations, that such heady sensibilities weren't for the likes of me. The girl I had been became my secret, private thing—the love I had felt for Dennis Mayo became the compelling determinant in my life. Oh, I was over him, I didn't dream of having him back; but he was my love memory, at least I knew I had loved someone.

It was my trick of staying alive. I called it up whenever I felt overwhelmed by the consequences of a detached heart. A decision made so young! Held to so fast!

Georgie swayed for a moment, then lowered herself carefully onto her very clean floor. She remembered the business at hand for this morning: she was going to kill herself.

And it would have to be done as only Georgie would do it, the aftermath clear in her mind so she could play it over, experience it, savor it. Suzanne, she knew, would weep, she would waken in the night filled with anguish, straining for the clues she should have read. Beth would want to shake her, thrash her back to life; perhaps beg Georgie's forgiveness for her moment with Dennis? But that would be ridiculous; it had nothing at all to do with Beth, it was just that she got caught.

Poor Lew, Georgie thought, it had nothing at all to do with him, either. Still she knew he would be dazed, stunned by the enormity of her loss as keeper of the sanctuary. He would probably feel awfully guilty for the part of him that was relieved, and the part of him that was embarrassed by what others might think *he* had done, for it to come to this.

Strange, but Georgie realized that their friends in the neighborhood, the couples with whom she and Lew had spent so much time over so many years, wandering like robots from dinner parties to cocktail parties, from patios to pools, brunches, barbecues . . . none of them were really close. But then what did they know of her, or she of them? Details, an accumulation of facts and statistics. Maybe now they'd piece it together, ahh, so *that's* who she was, poor thing.

The children. Well, not children anymore, she and Lew had got that right. Laura, her most practical child, her eldest, perceived more than she ever revealed and had, for some time now, been facing Georgie woman-to-woman. Laura would find a place to put this, and worry over her own emotional agility. And recognize in the end that Georgie had been counting on her to be the woman/daughter of the woman/mother.

Georgie cut the phone wires just in case she lost her nerve, and then she lost it completely. It suddenly seemed to her that the only reason she could be so moved by her own misery was that she wanted to live, she *cared* about her life

No she didn't; she didn't care at all. Here she was, over forty, okay, okay, forty-seven to be exact, ridiculously overweight, I mean who is this person, wallowing in a loveless marriage, playing at life, no future hopes, what, run off with Paul Newman? Yes, it's true I've centered everything on a man, my litany here is concerned with men, as if they could be the answer to anything; shall I become a rocket scientist?

She took the pills she'd been hoarding and lay down on her bed, waiting to feel something, then began to feel strangely calm, and then relieved. This was after all the last statement; there was no other statement she'd be called upon to make, thank God. She was already dead, anyway. But now at least she wouldn't have to fake her life, conjure it with potions, and sleights of hand. She suspected Beth and Suzanne were relying on magic lately as well, but they were not in her fix by a long shot, not by Georgie's account. She tried to remember exactly what her fix was, and felt herself floating, losing all sense of time, overtaken by the absence of need; safe in her hammock.

Slightly giddy, pleased with herself, Georgie decided that she deserved one last meal: that was the ritual, wasn't it? She made her way unsteadily back to the kitchen, found the chocolate cake and went at it clumsily with a knife, cutting herself. She dug into the cake with her fingers. It felt wonderful, but she had trouble navigating the chocolate to her mouth; some of it stuck on her cheek.

Now she wanted a cigarette. She hadn't smoked for months but she felt certain it was what one did after a meal. Lew kept a carton in the kitchen and she rummaged around the drawers until she found it. Opening a pack was a painstaking process with the drug taking hold, but she concentrated hard, willing herself this one last pleasure. No matches, how could there not be . . . Lew with his lighter, the fancy Dunhill she'd given him, her fault. She turned on the burner and leaned over it, remembering as she smelled her singed lashes that Lew used to admonish her to "hold the cigarette in your hand, for God's sake, when you do that!" Too late. She leaned against the wall, savoring the inhalation of smoke as the shock of it coursed through her system, and slipped down slowly, telling herself she'd rest just for a moment before getting back into bed.

The cigarette fell from her hand onto the tile floor and made an ugly yellow mark. The burner on the stove, still on, licked at the air and finally caught the fancy French potholders hanging nearby; they in turn set the wood cabinet to smoldering, slowly, until the curtains caught and burst into flames.

A neighbor coming from her garage out back saw the flames, ran to Georgie's door and rang the bell, knocked, pounded, then raced home and called the fire department.

When they found her, Georgie was bleeding profusely. She had nearly sliced off her thumb, and they assumed that was why she had passed out, but when they couldn't revive her she was taken to the emergency room at St. Mary's and her stomach was pumped, just in time. Or too soon, depending upon your point of view. And what a mess: fat lady smeared with chocolate cake botches suicide attempt, sets house on fire. Well, only the kitchen; fitting.

When she awoke there was a male intern leaning over her playing Ben Casey, whom he'd probably never heard of; she was grateful for his pained look, his studied, impersonal manner. The dry lines embedded in his forehead, belying his youth, made her think of the rocks she and Lew had seen once in Nevada. They'd attended a convention for Lew's business in Las Vegas, and quickly tired of it. The incessant flashing neon, the Midwestern ladies with their cups of quarters, their fat white arms hanging on the levers of the slot machines, the bordello decor of their room, all of it had driven them out into the vastness of Nevada. They rode for miles, the uninhabitable space stretching before them, startling their New York eyes. So it really was like this, burnt-out shrubbery, spindly trees, an occasional defiant dash of green, the land's screaming thirst like sand in your throat. Yet the rocks, arching toward the sky like mountains, were magnificent. Georgie couldn't take her eyes off them, and as they drove closer she was held by their dark beauty, the deeply etched lines time had burned into them, telling their stories in a language all their own.

"Wouldn't you like to be those rocks, to see what they've seen, to know what they know?" Georgie had said, hardly realizing the words had left her mouth, mesmerized by the inexplicable affinity she felt for the scene before them. And Lew had said, "What could they possibly have seen? Nothing happens here, nothing's *ever* happened here." And he'd laughed. She felt, at that moment, more completely alone than she could ever remember. She heard a low, steady murmuring coming from the rocks, or perhaps, as she thought later, she imagined it. She didn't say a word all the way back to their hotel, not out of pique but from a feeling of separateness; she knew the murmuring had been meant for her, it filled her head with longing.

Lew called Suzanne to break the news of Georgie's suicide attempt, and asked her to get to Beth—a lucky break on the off chance that Beth would blame herself, because of her sudden revelation about Dennis Mayo. But Beth knew, as Suzanne did, that they'd been losing Georgie for a long time; that it wasn't an old story that had done her in, but rather what she had lost in the years since, and what she perceived her life would be from this moment on.

Lew was devastated. Georgie was wrong, he didn't worry about what anyone might think, nor would he have been relieved if she had pulled it off. No, what this husband experienced was the realization of his deepest dread: his wife had chosen death over what they had together. The fact that she had botched it changed nothing.

The following morning Suzanne drove to Westchester to pack a suitcase of Georgie's clothes, as prearranged with Lew. It was Georgie's wish to stay in Manhattan for a short time, or rather, to be away from Lew for a short time, or rather, as Beth and Suzanne assured him, just to catch her breath. The man was dazed and in no condition to argue; there were no children at home to take care of; what counted was that Georgie was alive and would, at some point, be well.

Beth was to pick Georgie up at the hospital and take her back to her apartment. As she walked down the hall to Georgie's room, she heard the clatter of her own high heels and felt inappropriate in this sanctum, intrusive; more aware than ever of how close Georgie had come to the brink; how they had very nearly lost her. But there Georgie was, on her bed, already dressed. Her feet didn't touch the floor. She didn't seem to realize anyone was there. Then her eyes, pouchy and discolored as if she'd been in a fight, began to focus. Slowly, she raised her arms to Beth, who flew into them.

That evening, having settled Georgie in and put her to bed, Beth and Suzanne moved softly, as if any sound at all might be bruising. Then they sat, two edgy soldiers, their eyes on Georgie's door, prepared to guard her zealously from that recalcitrant villain, herself.

Each could have sworn they had been college roommates—children—only yesterday.

thirteen

Beth had been feeling particularly low, what with Robert gone (although she hadn't really wanted him to stay) and her miscarriage (although she hadn't really wanted to be pregnant); these decisions had been made for her, taken out of her hands while she stood wringing them. At least Georgie had *done* something. Oh yes, she'd gone and done it, all right. It was as sobering to Beth as a sharp slap; her own self-pity seemed a useless and indulgent luxury when someone she loved had such pain as to want to be done with life.

She wanted to be counted upon by Georgie, to be the linchpin on her road back to the living; quite by accident, she had a running start. Georgie had never shaken her capacity for delight and excitement in the accomplishments of her old friends . . . she had cheered Suzanne on for years, reveling in every commercial she produced, pointing out her work to everyone who would listen with the pride of a cackling hen; and of course she read every one of Beth's articles with a fervor bordering on the religious. So when television suddenly beckoned, in the form of a trial run for Beth on *The Morning Show,* Georgie felt herself rise up from her torpor like a sponge cake at 350 degrees. She claimed to have her thumb on the pulse of a portion of the *Morning* audience—the American housewife—despite her occasional deviation, her penchant for departure from the norm. And so, with the faintest hint of color in her cheeks, she discussed subject matter with Beth, who had been asked to read a short essay twice a week as if she was . . . well, talking it. Conversing. There was a rehearsal session or two before her first real appearance; just about enough to cause her to empathize, for the very first time, with Sally Quinn, ill-fated co-host of a morning news show whose reign was as short as her training.

From the beginning, Beth had found the world of television disconcerting. On the air, the set for *The Morning Show* appeared to have a depth, a plushiness, even a contrived warmth. Yet when she stood in front of it, she thought it looked like a wildly illuminated doll's house. In this arena, any notion of reality belonged in quotes.

She went through makeup on the first day with her nerves raw and her heart pounding. The piece she was going to "talk" rolled around in her head like alphabet soup at the boil. She thought of the absolute superiority every print journalist claimed over the Ken and Barbie dolls of the tube, unless offered the opportunity to join them, and knew it had its roots in pancake: the definitive mark of show business. Still, like everyone who had succumbed before her, Beth told herself she was not selling out, she was merely taking the opportunity to reach people who didn't read—who were, after all, the majority.

It had been a shock, after the dreamy serenity of the empty, early-morning streets, to walk into this beehive of activity; people were awake, dressed, moving, talking, eating, drinking, joking. One of the anchors, a dazzling blonde, came into the makeup room with huge rollers in her hair, a slightly bloody piece of floral-patterned Kleenex stuck to her chin, and a pout suggesting the temerity of a whitehead for having dared to invade. She glanced at Beth.

"Welcome to Wonderland."

Beth smiled hello, and took a sip of coffee.

"Easy on that, you'll have to pee."

The makeup woman moved the Clorets to one side of her mouth. "You think everyone's like you, one sip, unzip?"

"*She* knows," the anchorwoman said, gesturing to Beth.

And Beth did, squeezing her legs together at the thought.

The weatherman came in, looking perfect, sharing a joke with himself. He was a tall, thin man with white hair, unwrinkled, meticulous. On the air he seemed to be fighting a losing battle with a mind-altering substance, his voice dangerously high, standing on tiptoe as if straining to bite the moon. Watching him some mornings, Beth had the feeling he would break out in a maniacal cackle and have to be carted off, every hair in place. He betrayed none of this now, as he bowed to her in greeting.

A feature reporter came by, one of those Midwestern fellows with silky brown hair, serviceable glasses and an indistinguishable face, who spoke slowly and carefully about someone's goodness in Cheyenne or someone's plight in Racine, always with a tinge of wonder at what they had uncovered. They had first names that were last names, last names your tongue couldn't roll to from their first names, and a sense of purpose in their Izod uniform. Yet somehow they were never as penetrating or as quietly commanding as Charles Kuralt in a clerk's short sleeves.

There was a camaraderie among them, these early-rising morning stars, thrown together by a combination of research, gut signals, and executive whim, permitted or exhorted to stay by virtue of ratings that fluctuated just enough to keep the Maalox at a reasonable level and the attainment of the horizon in sight. Rumors flew through the production staff periodically, causing alarm or relief, fear or elation, depending upon one's camp. But the stories were generally old or ill-founded, like those that appeared in newspapers and magazines when a resident television expert charted the morning news wars.

By now the anchorwoman was in full bloom, her hair combed and sprayed into casualness, her face aglow with a harsh, excess layer of pancake, blush and eye color, which would soften under the lights, her lips gooey with gloss. Just like Beth. Except that Beth was unused to it, her face reminding her of the cherubs painted on the headboard of her childhood bed.

The anchorman was the last to arrive, causing an abrupt change in the atmosphere—tension hovered over him and moved with him like Pigpen's cloud of dirt. He held a rolled-up script in his hand, tapping his thigh with it; he sat in the makeup chair and drummed on the arms with his fingers. Short and compact, his walk was the insolent swagger of a man to whom all was simply due; whatever extent of all that had actually come to him he owed to the fact that the television audience always saw him sitting down. He was flashing his team-player grin, the one he'd been exhorted to adopt when research had determined that many thousands who no longer watched *The Morning Show,* as well as a significant percentage of those who still did, thought he was arrogant. Just how much of the audience he had convinced of the change in his personality was debatable; among his co-workers, there was a measurable desire for the return of J. Fred Muggs, infamous chimp of *Today* show fame who knew a good gig when he had one, and kept his grunts to a minimum.

What was she doing here?

Ah. Well.

She needed new beginnings.

Watching the co-hosts on the air from another room, Beth was struck at once by the apparent ease with which they spoke to America and to each other; even more so by their lack of alarm as they interviewed various personalities, experts in a variety of fields, even heads of state, armed only with prepared questions, unfettered by knowledge. Still, the famous and the powerful called them by their first names and suffered their persistence—which generally took the form of baldly trying to get others to misspeak—with the equanimity of a parent dealing with an overly precocious child.

When it was Beth's turn to appear, she listened to the welcoming introduction with the sickening sense that her accomplishments belied her true self, and that a good chunk of America would now find that out; but then, why would they care? It was small comfort, but it kept her tongue in motion for the whole of her commentary. And while she did not remember to blink, look down occasionally and look up sincerely, conscious only of the strange appendages that were her hands and the words on the TelePrompTer whose meaning escaped her, she did not flub.

When an engineer removed the microphone from her shirt, she had the presence of mind to cling to him as her means of escape, for to Beth the greatest feat of anyone who found himself on stage was getting off without being transformed into the bumbling Inspector Clouseau. Vinnie Palumbo, the lady-killer from Maspeth, wore his tightest jeans and his best manners as he led her safely through the minefield of cables and cameras, out of harm's way. When he gave Beth the "O" sign with his fingers, indicating a job well done, she longed to go home with him to his secure split-level elaborately wired for sound and listen to Wayne Newton's greatest hits. She had such feelings occasionally for cab drivers and cops who appeared, in a momentary brush, to be the men of her childhood dreams; they passed.

Having gotten through her trial run well enough, Beth was asked to appear every Monday and Thursday. Within a few weeks she began to be noticed on the street, "recognized," which happened so rarely in newspaper work that she was ill-prepared for it; stunned, in fact. Her name didn't matter, it hadn't yet registered, but her face was now part of that gallery of public images eagerly devoured by anonymous eyes that did not differentiate between the wealthy murderer and the Nobel Prize winner, the drag queen and the Prince of Peace. Once you were "someone," it was all the same.

Her mailbox was suddenly stuffed with invitations from people she didn't know but had sometimes heard of; with mail-order catalogs offering designer clothes and jewels; with charity pleas and speaking requests, letters from brokers, money managers, insurers, furriers, limousine services, caterers, masseurs, florists, pet cemeteries. She was someone. She was treated, at various restaurants, with an oozing obsequiousness, and while she reckoned that Claus von Bulow and Sidney Biddle Barrows engendered the same treatment, that the royalty she was now part of was as accidental and as sullied as it was celebrated, it beat waiting on line. She was having fun.

Harold Caso was the last person to whom she'd want to admit this. As the editor of the op-ed page of her paper, he'd been more than her mentor and champion, although that alone was rare enough; he'd been, in his dry, quiet way, her spiritual guardian, illuminating minefields at first, then crevices, then the trip wires of her own making that were the deadliest of all. Although she was part of the syndicated writers' group now, she still wrote to please Harold; his was the imprimatur she actively sought, but she wasn't likely to get it, not this time. Harold believed in the printed word with a fervor approaching evangelical zeal; he was not enamored of television. He likened the picture box to a stray mongrel on one's back porch whom a prudent man wouldn't trust, despite its plea for attention, its wagging tail.

She supposed he was a father substitute, and yet while their age difference had seemed like a chasm twenty years ago, there had been that curious catch-up you feel, even with parents, as you get to where they've been before you, and remember them there. When Beth met Harold he was in his early forties, looking very nearly the way he did today; he claimed that his hairline began receding, at his request, the moment its boundaries were set, due to his profound belief that aging was more easily handled when one was young.

Since her television debut, she had slunk in and out of the newsroom, delivering her columns to the writers' group editors, assiduously avoiding Harold. In all the years she'd known him, he'd made no direct inquiries about her personal life, he'd just assumed that she managed it all quite well. His view of her, on that level, was as someone beyond his scope, a shimmering specimen that swam in another sea, the waters of which were foreign to him. It wouldn't do for her to engage him in true confessions, to allow of mortal heartache or ordinary despair; to explain: I need this chintzy halo to stop the slide.

On this day, she would not have said, I've just learned Robert is seeing a woman half my age and I feel as if I've been hit on the head by a brick; I mourn, not for love lost, but for the shocking finality of this tired old path: youth gone. The rearrangement, the accommodation of all parts to the inevitable.

What is most difficult is the vanity itself, its degrading quality. We see the world through men's eyes, Harold; most of us. Because we *need* men. How are we supposed to believe that age doesn't matter, when we are reminded in every possible way that it does? You would call this, from afar, intellectual bankruptcy, but it is really intellect betrayed: what the mind says has absolutely nothing to do with the reality of this man's world.

And you would say to me, if we spoke of Robert, How can this possibly affect you? How can you place judgment in the hands of a man who prefers a child to a woman? How can you allow *any*one's view to mark you, to change you in your own eyes? Surely only you can lose the woman you are.

Beth walked into Harold's office and discussed the new world of television. He was kind enough to listen.

fourteen

Neal hunched against the window of the taxi, knees up, holding his overcoat like an awkward package. He never looked quite right in that coat, rather like a boy wearing his father's hand-me-down that didn't yet fit. They'd gotten a Checker when they didn't need one, and so Suzanne felt she was sitting across a sea from him. She could see the knots in his thighs through the proper blue suit as they rode in silence to the airport.

It was unseemly somehow to bear witness to such wildly apparent apprehension in the man she loved. Neal wanted this new job with a desperateness that surprised her, not for the feeling itself but for his inability to control it, to rein it in. She knew he was ambitious, that work was a serious endeavor, even at times a deadly game, but she'd never been privy to the wanting before, and hadn't any idea what her part should be. He must want her to have a part—that was why he'd insisted she ride with him to the airport. But she could think of nothing to say that would be right, not even an attitude that would soften this picture: the man unmoving, electric with agitation, the woman concerned at her uselessness and yet savoring the glint of relief she felt at the notion that he was flying away.

It was her own curious relationship with John Hanna that had brought Neal to this. John had been Suzanne's first real client at the agency. His company had then consisted of a small band of wunderkinds, his "boys," he called them, wizards from M.I.T. and Carnegie Tech, who saw, as he did, the extraordinary possibilities of the aerospace industry. The company's first breakthrough had been a minuscule chip that greatly enhanced rocket trajectory; from there they'd designed nose cones, lasers, a variety of space-industry products, until now they were big business. But John, the businessman among them, had kept his nucleus, his team, intact. That was his trademark: he demanded and engendered loyalty.

Creating trade ads back then as a junior art director, Suzanne had had few opportunities to shine. But the copywriter on John's account had been content to write from a bare surface knowledge, whereas Suzanne had eagerly immersed herself in John's business, believing that the more she understood, the more effective her ads would be. John Hanna had been impressed; he was dazzled, if the truth be told, not only by her enthusiasm, her vibrancy, but by the sheer force of her. He had recognized, from the first, her odd combination of gutsiness and emotional fragility; he could appreciate and attend to her separate parts with equal ease; he'd fallen in love with her. He loved her still, but with a vague contentedness. Their one attempt at ardor had been bittersweet; it was all under control now, put away in its proper, workable place. John had been married to Patsy Hanna for thirty years.

The company was based in Boston, but John made frequent trips to New York. His friendship with Suzanne had deepened steadily as he moved from being mentor to father confessor until, finally, they were equals. He was as proud of her success as he'd be of a daughter's, and yet he was able to bridge that gulf and welcome her to his turf with open arms.

At dinner three weeks ago, John had mentioned that he was in pursuit of an executive vice president, another business head to back him up and perhaps eventually take over the company. He had just experienced, for the second time, the failure of a possible successor, and was feeling overburdened. As he laid out the requirements for the job, Suzanne immediately thought of Neal—and suddenly realized how very alike the two men were with regard to their work. Both were naturally suspicious, shrewd maneuverers, unusually quick. Where they differed was in style: Neal's business face was polished, slick, at times arrogant; he relied on humor to gain forgiveness. John's patina was mottled from his years as a boy in the streets; tough as he was, he was direct, unfiltered—and therefore trusted. John had met Neal only twice, each time in a social setting, and so she was surprised at his definitive reading.

"He's a killer," John said bluntly. "I don't know if I'm comfortable with that."

"What do you mean exactly?" Suzanne asked, as if his answer would solve the riddle of her own connection with Neal.

"He's bright, I'll give you that; sharp as hell. But so damned political you'd never be sure if he was doing something for you or to you." He pursed his lips. "What's so funny?"

"You're describing yourself," she said, not at all delicately.

He roared with laughter.

The two men had met several times in the days that followed, and now Neal was on his way to an on-site conference and tour. It was done, she knew, the job was Neal's, but of course she couldn't tell him that—anymore than she could tell him of the lines of persuasion she had used with John Hanna to seal it at the onset. It wasn't that John was doing it for her, precisely; business was business. Yet he was doing it because of her, because he trusted her judgment and her instincts, knowing that she cared as much about him, in her way, as she did about Neal.

They arrived at the airport and made their way to the shuttle gate. Neal stood shaking his head.

"I'm nervous as hell," he said. She thought if she touched him, springs would pop out. Her own discomfort was extreme; she wanted him gone. It was such an entirely new feeling she thought it might release her to the air, like a child's errant balloon. He bent to kiss her, his face softening for an instant.

"I love you. Call you the minute it's over."

She blew a kiss as he turned to board the plane, and watched the stiffness of his walk until he was no longer visible and she was watching strangers. It seemed entirely possible, at that moment, that any one of them might be the man she thought he was, that any one of them might have said or done the very thing that had drawn her to him, that even the air might have contrived to toss her giddily into that pair of arms, or that one. Instead, Neal was the one she had found or been found by, his was the face she sought in a crowd, the being with whom she had come to be connected. Now he was going to Boston. Away.

But hadn't he always been away, from her? Was this really so different? His wife wasn't going with him; perhaps only because she adamantly refused to leave New York or perhaps because she and Neal were separating for good this time, Neal having had a hand in the decision; perhaps this was his definitive move toward Suzanne? Her ability to decipher specifics had atrophied, just as her obsessive eye's perpetual squint at the future had obscured its peripheral view. Neal saw to it. He was going to find a rambling brownstone apartment with room for all of them, for Suzanne and the kids, and send for them when he got settled. Suzanne knew the plan because they had discussed it, "just in case this opportunity of a lifetime comes through." What they hadn't discussed were the details, such as selling her apartment, schools for the children, her own career; what they hadn't addressed was what effect such a move would have on them, on her children, his marriage, her life: small print, loose change. Neal preferred that they remain afloat, their future a magical, ethereal thing, and Suzanne, curled up in a ball of sublime selflessness, had been in no condition to offer resistance.

But it no longer seemed real. Real life was her son Daniel's wet dreams, with his father 2,000 miles away; it was the incessant winnowing of her parents' friends, picked off by an impatient, often cruel God; or a barely recognizable Georgie, inching her way back to hopefulness. Real life was the insistence of the managing partners at Suzanne's agency that no merger was in the offing, despite rampant rumors which they attributed to common paranoia and the trade papers ascribed to unusually reliable sources. It was real life that kept Suzanne awake these nights, not Neal.

At seven that evening he called from the airport to tell her he'd gotten the job. "This never would have happened without you, and I know it. God, I love you, and honey, don't worry; everything will be perfect now."

His voice went on, wonderfully warm and boyish, flooding her perception of how perfectly imperfect "everything" was.

fifteen

Georgie had lost weight—in her face, of course—where else do you lose when your hips bulge and your thighs roll? Each morning she'd look in the bathroom mirror and see a thin, overtired countrywoman of indeterminate age who could still fill in the crevices and polish the surface for an evening out. Then she'd turn to the full-length glass on the bathroom door for the Big Surprise. She did this religiously, no artist or writer she; no make-believe. Her periods had stopped.

Well once, she'd skipped once. Probably the pills, Beth said. Probably true. Cold all the time now, as if her body had received the signal of death only to have its circuits jammed, she thought even hot flashes would be an improvement.

Beth hovered; given her crazy hours because of *The Morning Show,* she lent new meaning to the word. She was away when Georgie slept and there when Georgie was up, and had she been Lew, Georgie would have killed her by the second week. The young Georgie would have relished the daylight presence of Dennis Mayo, her soon-to-be-sung hero, tapping away at his typewriter in the next room, while she, eyes bright with belief, kept their digs in order. But this was the old Georgie; older. The Georgie who fed on the silence of rooms, a life of her own design.

Nothing was in place anymore. Beth ignored invitations for weeks, as if she had a sick child, an invalid to tend. The one night she gave in, a cocktail party honoring Harold Caso, Suzanne had been dispatched for duty. Artfully, of course: just dropped by. Georgie was impatient at their presence and brooded in their absence; she hated the clicking sound of that ugly black machine, Beth's old Royal, hated its fits and starts and bloody bell, signal of life; she hated the sound of her own breathing even more.

They talked about it only once. Georgie tried to head them off, but Beth and Suzanne were as presumptive as only old friends can be; she was no match for them. Even as she attempted to limit their concern to the question of whether or not she was a candidate for a retake, they were having none of it. Georgie was the sort who wound herself up for things, a top that sprung, and they knew it; the required energy, the required thought, the sense of purpose, desire itself, were all gone; even dying was too much of an effort. And so no pills were flushed, no knives removed, no fail-safe precautions of any kind were taken at Georgie's latest hideout; for Beth's apartment had merely been substituted for Georgie's home in Larchmont, and they knew that too. It was just that without Lew there, and without the people and habits of her suburban world to keep her functional, Georgie could give herself up completely to her inner life.

What they weren't sure of, as perhaps one never can be regarding anyone else, was what combination of thoughts and feelings, what wounds, what old dreams could have plunged this friend they'd known and loved since girlhood into such despair. They made Georgie talk, but they couldn't make her tell. She was too ashamed at having sunk so low, at having proved so weak—where were her "good" reasons, the sort that were debated on the *Donahue Show?* And she was loathe to admit her overwhelming feeling of hopelessness, as that had gotten her into this in the first place. Georgie's plan was to remain numb, for there lay safety. Yet this was precisely what she had done in her marriage, and it hadn't worked. Now Beth and Suzanne insisted on stirring the pot where her emotions stewed, determined that it wouldn't work this time either.

Georgie had been lolling around at Beth's for more than three weeks, when, on a mild, nearly springlike Saturday, she was exhorted to get dressed, which she knew, crafty as ever, meant going out. She did not resist, if only to surprise her old friends, keep them on their toes. It was her first time in the open since she'd left the hospital. The air smelled surprisingly sweet—deceptive, she thought—making her feel that the residue of her former self, like the safety tank in a gas guzzler, still hadn't run dry. She and Beth strolled through the park arm in arm, after which they were to go to Suzanne's for brunch. Georgie recognized a regimen coming: first you exercise, then you eat.

Dale was at Suzanne's when they arrived. Georgie had met

him only once before, and had liked him instantly, each of them so good at covering up. Now she felt embarrassed, for it was she who had broken under the strain; was that it? Was he there for therapy too, like treating like? But the children were there as well, Daniel and Annie, and so she was safe after all.

Suzanne brought forth a sumptuous platter of bagels, smoked salmon, tomatoes and onions, and Daniel, as if on cue, begged Georgie to prepare eggs ranchero, which "Mom makes all messy." And so she did; wily kid.

When Georgie served her neat treasure, done by rote, Suzanne turned on the awe and turned to Dale.

"See what I mean?" she said. Georgie ignored this.

Dale smiled and nodded, stabbing a forkful.

"Am I right?" Suzanne said, Georgie not looking.

Dale smiled and nodded. And swallowed. He turned to Georgie. "I have this friend," he began.

"Who can't cook?" Georgie said.

"Well, not exactly. He's a food photographer. You know, like those ads for Kraft where they slop mayonnaise on everything till you want to throw up?"

"Eeew!" Annie said.

"Beg pardon, my sweet. In any event, food photography is an art. Of a sort. You can't imagine the care that's taken, how perfectly each dish must be prepared, the lighting, the setting."

"For everything under the sun slopped in mayo?" Georgie said, as flippantly as she could manage, wondering wildly if there could possibly be a job in the offing, charity with a capital C. And here she was, barely recovering from a walk in the park. Were they crazy? Was she? Was that it?

"Even that. He's a free-lance, a specialist. He can pick and choose who he works with and I thought . . . it occurred to me that . . ." Dale looked at Suzanne for help.

"Georgie, you'd be perfect," Suzanne pronounced.

"You mean to say he'd hire me just because Daniel likes my eggs ranchero?" Georgie asked. Daniel beamed.

"Why not?" Dale said. "It isn't as if you're not qualified; you cook extraordinarily well, and that means you know food, you understand it. And what's wrong with taking advantage of a contact, it's done all the time. Hell, most of the time. Why not you?"

"But it's crazy. I don't know the first thing about cameras, lighting . . ." Georgie looked helpless, agitated.

"That's his job, not yours. What the food stylist worries about is making the burgers look mouthwatering and keeping the cookies from crumbling when they're munched, maybe even coating the ham with Karo syrup to make it glisten. You'd be the food stylist's assistant, which means you'll get to learn how to do that."

"Look, I know what you're trying to do and I appreciate it," she lied, "but it's too soon, really."

"It's not too soon. In fact it's probably long overdue," Beth said. "And this is *per*fect for you."

Georgie looked at Beth, then Suzanne, and decided not to argue, so as to soothe their fervor while she figured how to get out of this.

"You have time, you know," Suzanne said. "The photographer's in Ireland, on vacation for three weeks."

"County Mayo?" Georgie asked.

They grinned at her, relieved. Georgie taken care of, set out on a new life! Georgie herself was relieved, at her three-week reprieve; given time, Georgie figured she could get out of anything.

The phone rang and Daniel answered, then called out to Dale. Suzanne looked alert.

"It's Noel someone," Daniel said.

"Whitehead?" Suzanne asked.

Daniel nodded. "I think so."

Dale looked at Suzanne as if to gird himself, then went to the phone and walked with it as far as the line would extend so that his voice came back to them as a murmur.

Beth squinted thoughtfully. "Noel Whitehead. Do I know that name? Doesn't he work with, what is it, Bill Haverly? Who does the advertising column? Suze?"

"Umm," Suzanne said, half listening.

"Is something going on at the agency?" Beth asked. Suzanne shrugged and Beth let it drop for the moment, but her mind was racing. She had recently written an article on the latest version of white-collar crime: companies sold, sometimes even undersold, right out from under their employees and their stockholders, for the sole and extraordinarily substantial benefit of their top officers. Advertising agencies were hardly exempt, and in fact recent megamergers were considered by some to be harmful to clients as well as personnel, which was of course unforgivable. In her piece, Beth had searched for examples of ethical considerations in these 1980s arrangements, and had come up dangerously close to empty. She had talked with Suzanne at the time about Damon & Moore, because she'd heard rumors of a possible merger. But as Suzanne had said, the stories had been floating around for months, and were denied vigorously at every turn by the managing partners. Suzanne had also said she knew that meant little, but it got you through the week.

Dale was back, affecting a casual air. "Well, it's done," he said to Suzanne. "They'll announce next week." He sat down and began working assiduously on a bagel, building layers of cream cheese, salmon, tomatoes and onions, as if there was a prize to be had for neatness and symmetry.

They ate. The moment dragged and finally passed, even some degree of merriment was restored. Then Annie was off to a friend's house and Daniel was happily closed up in his room, and Suzanne felt free to sigh heavily. But why be concerned; wasn't she moving to Boston after all? Leaving Damon & Moore behind? It was going to be a new life with Neal, in a new place, and that meant a new job. She'd even begun preparing the children for Boston, Neal having assured her they'd all be moving soon. But the "soon" had yet to be specified, and she feared that she had inadvertently hoisted her kids onto the pendulum she had been riding alone for years. Neal flicked at it, she swung. But her children were not so accommodating. They both felt a natural anxiety at the prospect of leaving their friends and moving to a strange city, but it was Neal's connection, the fact that Neal was triggering the move, that opened the floodgates. Daniel flailed at his mother like an itchy prosecutor: was she sure they were going? When were they going? Was it definite? How did she know? Then Annie's baby face, her woman's eyes, had turned on Suzanne like a whip, her lips pursed in helplessness: Neal had worn her out with his coming and going.

Suzanne had reached out automatically and patted at them, her wary children, missing them altogether. And slid back under Neal's crazy quilt. She told herself it would be all right once they got to Boston, and she prepared to make herself believe it as if readying for a ritual ablution. Then talk heated up about a merger at the agency, and suddenly Suzanne recognized the possibility that she didn't believe in Boston any more than her children did. Her stake was here, at Damon & Moore; her life was here, in New York. Oh, if Neal wanted her to move, if he made the offer definitively, she would not turn him down. But the reality was that as yet he hadn't. The reality was that he was still holding the carrot—the ultimate profession of his love—just beyond her reach, for which she, obsessive and dreamy, had allowed her children to pay. She could still fog up at the sound of Neal's voice, his soothing patter; she could still imagine their idyll and could even summon up a passionate belief in the rightness of their union. But from the instant of her children's reaction to the move she had begun to reckon with the possibility of being without him by her own choice. Always, in the past, it had been the prospect of his reactions, his feelings, his perceptions that had occupied her. This was new; she wished to hold on to it.

Dale was saying good-bye, hugging her as he whispered in her ear that they'd talk later. Now, gratefully, there was business at hand; there was Georgie.

"What you need," Beth said to Georgie, "is a whole new wardrobe, now that you're going to be a working girl."

"What I need is a whole new body."

Suzanne grinned at her. "That too."

Georgie looked from one to the other. "Oh. Hey . . ."

"Oh yes," Beth said, with finality.

Georgie put both hands out in front of her. "I tried fat farms, okay? They don't work, not for me. I tried Weight Watchers, Pritikin, high protein, low cholesterol, the champagne diet, the grapefruit diet, bananas, even that chalk you drink from a can!"

"Have you tried not eating?" Suzanne asked.

Georgie gave her a wide-eyed innocent look. "You mean death? I seem to recall . . ."

"Not funny," Beth said.

Georgie tried to look appropriately contrite while summoning the energy for one last appeal. "What do I have to get thin for? Who'll see me? I'm the cooker, right? Can't the cooker look as if she eats? Doesn't that make sense?" At their silence, she curled her lips like a fish pressed against a bowl. "Thin, huh?"

"Let's just say, thinner," Suzanne said. "As in healthy, not anorexic. What are you doing!"

"Food for the condemned," Georgie said, as she built a bagel sandwich. "I've always believed in it." She overdid her creation, turned it into a Dagwood Bumpstead special and took a huge bite, knowing it wouldn't be her last. Knowing too, with sudden clarity, that she had left Lew; Beth and Suzanne having accepted it, it must be so. She was no longer in that nether land of recovery, she was expected to plan, act, live. It seemed she'd be doing it here, in Manhattan—not in Larchmont, not with Lew, at least not now. She had said, from the hospital, that she couldn't go back there, that she needed time, now that she'd bungled and had time. Lew agreed. Well, of course, he always agreed. Still, hadn't she provided drama, finally? Not some little secretary, but Drama! The specter of Death! She'd awakened Lew, all right; she'd let him know that her life with him was unbearable, and then left him to deal with it as best as he could, while she . . . what? Put herself back together? Nor was Lew the only one her little production had touched; her children were finding ways to blame themselves, despite her protestations. And here were her dearest friends, trying everything they knew to get her out of the dark hole that had nearly swallowed her up, while she sat back exuding condescension like some smart-mouthed adolescent.

Done in by her list of grievances against herself, Georgie slumped down in her chair. "I'll do it, okay? I'll do it."

She took another huge bite of her Bumpstead bagel.

"What exactly is it I'm going to do?"

sixteen

Tired of lugging her expectations around, Suzanne went to Boston to see Neal. She hadn't precisely invited herself so much as nudged the invitation out of him. She had said, on the heels of his having told her he loved her, and missed her terribly, that they ought to consider seeing each other, there being airlines and trains and all sorts of possible ways to do this. And Neal had said yes, absolutely, how about this weekend?, as if she'd just hacked out the Oregon Trail and presented him with the map. It was the kind of conversation women know about, where you get what you thought you wanted only to realize you've already lost. She went anyway, because whatever she knew or was coming to know was still overshadowed by the desire for love—with this man, with Neal. And because the habit of her loving him, for all its unfulfilled promise, had become part of the mechanism that spurred her daily life.

She was nervous dressing for the trip. Everything had to be exactly right and nothing was. Her hair was suddenly dull and stubborn, her complexion sallow, she popped a button on her blouse and then couldn't thread the needle to sew it back on. She started over, put on a dress, painted luster on her face from a jar and saw her eyes look back at her, lifeless.

On the plane she tried not to smoke, but the effort caused her to smoke too much, deadening her senses. She welcomed it; what was there to think about, beyond Neal's old tune, her own persistent dance? Only her work, her career, her livelihood: Damon & Moore, the agency where she'd toiled and blossomed for over twenty years, had just "merged" with an agency more than twice its size. She was angry with the lot of them, with Bud Damon and Frank Moore and all the other principals, with Bernie, Enrico, Kevin and Phil; they'd all lied through their teeth, persuading everyone, most especially those who'd been with them long enough to have helped build the place, that Damon & Moore was not up for grabs. Up for gobbling was more like it; the agency would probably be eaten alive. Only Bud and Frank, and Bernie, Enrico, Kevin and Phil, those newly fatted calves, were assured of being on no one's plate.

In the taxi on the way to Neal's apartment, Suzanne concentrated on Boston, remembering herself as a half-grown child come to visit on college weekends, remembering wet, numbing kisses and grabby hands as she squirmed to keep her body's secrets; saving herself for true love.

Neal lived in a high rise of no particular character, surrounded by brownstones that offered the sort of apartments he had spun tales about to Suzanne. The doorman questioned her, an unknown intruder, then waved her in. She stepped from the elevator to find Neal out in the hall to greet her and take her bag. Once inside, he hugged her, but she found no comfort pressed against him. It was as if the curves she knew by heart, that could fold her in and warm her, had been mysteriously leveled out; only flat hard surfaces remained. She wanted to crawl inside him right then, if only to find him; instead, she struggled for control, as if to distance herself from the unraveling of her life. At Damon & Moore a colleague had calculated that their newly merged shop, run by people whose loyalties lay elsewhere, now had more redundancies in personnel than the federal government. She had laughed then, they all had, flexing their mettle. Now she smiled as she would have for a photo, the strain of posing having caused a barely perceptible quiver in her lips. Neal offered her a glass of wine.

"You look wonderful," he said.

"Thank you, I feel wonderful," she said.

She noticed the ashtrays were filled with cigarette butts. Neal explained he had held marathon meetings here during the week, the last of them having ended shortly before she arrived. He spun out his game plan, his approach with his managers, summoned up postures and postulates as he had countless times, awaiting her sanction, her wise counsel. She made a halfhearted attempt, but it was beside the point.

Neal smelled faintly of sweat. He was wearing an old football shirt and jeans, the outfit he had worn for his meeting, she was sure; he believed in teams, captains. He had small eyes, a small nose, thin lips, his chest was oddly concave, a bald spot was appearing at the crown of his head, his wiry copper hair was tamed. She was suddenly filled up with her love for him, even as she felt it sliding from her like some thick, muddy layer that had insulated her from the cold, from despair. She wanted to hold him, to be held; instead she rearranged herself, tucked her legs up as if to hide her heart.

He asked about Damon & Moore.

She didn't want to talk about it.

She said, "It's become an old story, this takeover business," acting like an amiable stranger.

"Besides," Neal said, "you don't have to worry, your talent is special. Wonderful and special." He beamed at her; blindly, she thought, or she'd have seized upon it as proof of his love. What was happening; what *had* happened? She was leaning forward, aware that her life had changed.

"I've been painting," she said.

"You've always painted."

"No, what I mean is I'm going to have a show."

"What?"

"At a gallery."

"Suzanne!"

"Dale did it. He just got it into his head when he saw what I'd been working on, and he didn't even tell me, he said I never would have let him take those paintings if I knew he was showing them to anyone at all, much less to Paul Salazar, that I would have told him he was crazy . . ."

"Salazar!" Neal said. "Even I've heard of him." He looked at her, waiting for the next surprise like a played-out child.

"Don't overblow this. He liked a few things, that's it. That's all." But of course it wasn't, not by half; she hadn't called Neal to tell him the moment it happened, any more than she had said she'd best put out feelers to agencies in Boston right away, before the expected upheaval at Damon & Moore—which could leave her out in the cold. This was not a woman talking to her lover, her best friend, although she knew they'd once had parts in such a play. She was looking at Neal expectantly, her eyes wide, imagining that one or the other of them would say, Where are we? I seem to have lost my place.

But Neal said, "Tired?"

And Suzanne said, "Yes." Oh, yes.

She put on her black lace nightgown because it was the one he loved; she thought to clean her face and was suddenly wary of finding herself out. She brushed her hair.

He had found *The Tonight Show* and was folding shorts and T-shirts and socks newly washed; she was surprised by the prissiness of his movements. Finished with the laundry, he gestured with pride to the shelves in his closet, swollen with the fruits of his very own labor. They settled in his queen-sized bed, the one he said he had bought for them, in the bedroom he said was just right for them, in the apartment he had picked out for them.

Neal was exhausted from having held late meetings all week; she knew this, and tried to be sympathetic as he stared at the set, inviting its dullness to envelop him and wind him down, which somehow it could; she knew this too. But she didn't feel sympathetic, even charitable.

He took her hand. And let it go to take a sip of melted ice and Scotch. And forgot to put it back.

He snorted his sinus honk.

He fell asleep.

Johnny Carson stared Bennyesque, a ferret on his head. She lay still, her eyes darting, focusing nowhere. A horn blasted, setting free the murder in her heart.

She thought, if I had a knife, I could do it now, kill the killer! A mother, an executive, a sensible woman, she got up instead, and made her way to the living room with the last of her wine.

She switched on the lights. What did she think of this place he said was meant for her? She who prided herself on her house-hunting ability, her keen eye for comforting corners, rounded edges, safe harbors, walked around in a daze. Furniture from his marriage had been put where it fit; literally, where there was room to put it. A lampshade was hopelessly frayed. She liked the apartment's high ceilings, the archways leading from room to room, especially the long hallway that separated the entrance from the life within, a city need. But what life within? This was not a home. A way station perhaps, curiously impersonal and uninviting. She could see them at Sloane's, Neal and his wife as newlyweds, deciding who they would be; choosing neo-Williamsburg. Suzanne and Mark had not done this, set pieces eluded them, their home had been a grab bag of varying moods. But Neal lived by design.

She forced herself to keep peeling off the outer skin of this man—merely a man!—who had recklessly puffed her up beyond reason, then let go of the string of the balloon. She had never seen him fold his socks before. He had never seen her reading in bed, hand cradled around a box of Wheat Thins. Visitors never see.

She saw dust on table tops; waiting for me, she thought. But nothing here is mine, there is nothing of me here. The pale blue couch, faithful copy of a period piece, its silk worn by ever-shifting backsides straining to find a curve, a groove, reminded her of the dollhouse museum she had found for Annie when they still lived in the country; Annie holding her hand tight, primed for adventure. Suzanne had already met Neal, her own adventure had begun and she had greeted it with a child's delight.

She shivered. How was it possible that all this time had

passed and she had missed the point? Her purest art was self-delusion.

Neal wandered into the living room and found her. Rubbing his head, blinking from the light, his shorts clean and blue, he said, "I can't believe I did that." Boyishly, he held out his arms. When she didn't seem about to move into them he whispered, "Forgive me?" And she did move, she moved across the room and up against him because she didn't know yet how not to. She let him hold her tight, tighter, because inside her was a deep black hole, black death pounding wildly at her. She let him lower them to the floor and even stroked his back, his legs, his thighs while he touched her everywhere, licked at her everywhere, pressed himself between her burning thighs and strained to fill her. She made believe he had because it didn't matter; because she knew that none of this could be allowed to matter anymore. Madness was only lack of recognition.

When Suzanne got back home she took the kids out for pizza. The Formica table top, the smell of cardboard, the Pepsi glasses and the sauce on the corners of their mouths made her feel like a woman comfortably in charge of her brood, her life, out on a spring night.

As she put the key in the door she heard the phone ringing and knew it was Neal. With the children hopping anxiously around her, she moved in slow motion, trying to wait him out. Finally the ringing stopped.

"Thanks a lot," Daniel said.

Her own sentiments exactly.

seventeen

When Beth first saw Terrence O'Neil she felt compelled to look again. His hair was of the unruly, fiery red generally found on small children with freckle-stained faces and on older women wearing hoop earrings. Even in his seat he seemed to tower over everyone; she imagined he was six-four or six-five. Clearly, he had never slouched out of awkwardness. He might have stood his ground once too often: his nose, prominent enough to be a target, had a bump just below the bridge, and another above the tip, making it appear slightly off center. His body had yielded to nothing. He was thin, muscular, beautifully proportioned; she knew this because his shirt fit him like a second skin, which suggested he knew it too. She would have said, hypothetically, that a man who dressed with such self-consciousness had an ego of unattractive proportion, a foppish bent. Looking at this red-haired giant, she thought nothing of the sort.

It seemed impossible she had missed him at the benefit concert, no matter the size of the hall. Now, at a late supper with friends, or what passed for friends in this circle of celebrity that had opened up just enough to let her step in, Beth found herself sitting across from him. She hadn't any idea who he was, and no one bothered to tell her; it was assumed everyone knew one another, among these people who knew everyone.

As the gossip and small talk flew around the table, he caught her eye and smiled, shaking his head in mild dismissal; as if to say, you and I are above all this, but still, it's nice to be here. Once the conversation turned to the theater, she began to piece together who he was—of course! Terrence O'Neil, director of the City Theater Club, the genius who had chosen, mounted and launched some unusually fine plays that were now thriving on Broadway and Off. He was considered, among those who knew, which surely included everyone present, to be one of the few who might successfully resurrect the theater, or at least rescue it from its current malaise. She was impressed. At some point he addressed her by name and told her he was a great fan, never making it clear if he actually knew what she did. It didn't bother her in the least, nothing did, until he left long before the others, begging off on the grounds of a heavy day coming up. She missed him immediately and was relieved, immediately, when he left alone.

He found time to call her the next day. Two nights later, at dinner, they took turns talking and eating, listening intently. He, for example, threw dates around like cherry bombs—graduation from college in '75, Yale Drama in '77—causing her the great discomfort of realizing he was at least fourteen years younger than she was. It occurred to her that in certain countries girls routinely give birth at fourteen; she felt fortunate not to live in one. She berated herself that of course she had known he was younger; on the other hand, five or six years had seemed likely, maybe seven . . . good God, he probably didn't know who The Shadow was. Even worse, A-bomb drills, where you dove under your desk with your dog tag jiggling and your heart racing, were something he'd read about in a history book, or maybe seen in one of those quaint newsreels from before he was born. She wondered how she might have guessed, but this was an era where grown-ups, as soon as they realized they had to, took such good care of themselves that for a certain number of years they were, in terms of age, nearly indistinguishable . . . simply *them*, the ones who were no longer kids or young adults. Terrence, she now knew, still was a young adult, but then what was he doing with that face? What she had thought was mere weathering perhaps was character, or then again, genes.

She had stopped worrying over the accordian pleats ironing themselves into her pants. He had stopped talking.

He asked her, "Is anything wrong?"

"Not at all," she said, in the voice of a woman wearing white gloves and a hat. "Why would you think that?"

"Because," he said reasonably, "you've put clamshells in your salad bowl and there's a red dot on your cheek that wasn't there before."

"Oh, that," she said, meaning the red dot, retrieving the clamshells neatly. "Is it still there?" She rubbed lightly at her cheek, at precisely the spot. He nodded, smiling at her with such clear affection that she felt, through her fingers, the generation of heat on her cheek. "My father could always make me blush," she said, "and it pleased him that the only visible sign of it was a funny red dot on one cheek, which no one else seemed to notice. It became a secret between us, one of those private, special things that make no sense whatever, but keep you bound together."

"How did he do that?" Terrence asked, leaning forward. "Make you blush, I mean."

"Oh, he'd compliment me lavishly, outrageously." It occurred to her that this sounded like a cue for Terrence to do the same, which she rushed to cover. "Fathers are not particularly given to realistic appraisal where their daughters are concerned. In fact, they're notoriously myopic."

"Do you think it's the same with mothers and sons?" he asked.

"Never having been either . . . you'll have to tell me," Beth said, not really lying.

"I didn't get the chance to find out," Terrence said, averting his eyes for the first time, breaking the spell. "By the time I was four, my mother was gone. You're wincing at the thought of an early death, but it wasn't that; she left, walked out. There were three of us. I was the youngest. It took a while for it to sink in that she was really gone, really not coming back. Years later, when the feminist movement was at its height, I tried to look at what she'd done more kindly; maybe she was just ahead of her time, running for her life when it wasn't fashionable or even acceptable. But I never really believed that, it was an intellectual exercise, a stab at male sensitivity to the female plight; much too close to home." He brushed at the table with his pinkie, gathering up stray salt crystals and working them into a small mound. Beth said nothing. When he looked up it was as if he suddenly remembered her presence, his luck. "It's just a ploy, of course. Works wonders on women with mothering instincts."

She realized he had gotten far more personal than he normally permitted; she had sensed his embarrassment. Still, she was pleased at his exposure; it signified trust, even if it was only subconsciously felt. She herself had talked and talked, and revealed nothing in kind, her usual patter. The difference was, she wanted to . . . the difference was, for the first time in more years than she could remember, what she had to tell needed telling, and she knew she would eventually hand it over, her history, her story, with its banalities and fateful twists, to this particular man, for no particular reason that she could articulate, other than the oldest, and for her, most incomplete reason; she was starting to love him. She had started to love others, and yet had not been so tempted to lay herself bare.

Beth had put her hand on his.

"It wasn't all that bad," he said, reaching his fingers over hers. "The truth is, it brought us closer together than we might have been, my sisters and I, my father with all of us. I have more happy memories than sad ones. Besides," he said, grinning, his composure regained, "I knew it wouldn't work on you."

He took her to his home, the upper half of a brownstone in Brooklyn Heights, on an old street where the brass doorhandles and knockers didn't all gleam and the trees hung heavy. Trailing through it, Beth found the rooms a mixture of comfort and precision: the Indian rugs and deep chairs were inviting, yet one had the feeling they were nailed to the floor. There was, all at once, the temptation to sprawl and the suggestion that it really wouldn't do. She didn't know whether this reflected a personality at war with itself, or with the woman who had helped him decorate.

On his own, he was extraordinarily neat. Everything was in its clearly delineated place, the one sign of clutter a stack of books set against a wall in his study. Above it, the shelves were lined with hundreds of books, records and scripts. Otherwise, there was almost a Spartan quality to the place; he was not a collector, a pack rat, a storer—corners were bare, surfaces visible and clear.

It might have been a seduction scene like any other, but for the fact that he brought her to his home because of a feeling as irrational as it was overwhelming: that even her fleeting presence there would somehow permanently alter it. And because he wanted to make love to her.

She imagined that when they made love it would be on top of the bedspread, and only after Terrence had hung up his pants and shirt and folded his socks in his shoes; that his skin would feel cool and dry even when her own glistened with sweat, curling her hair.

She was wrong.

Their clothes were flung everywhere, the bed torn apart; they lay together joyously, soaked. It was an odd thing: she felt she had come to a place she always knew existed, as one knows death exists. You don't think about it because it may cause dizziness, slow you down, even stop you in your tracks when you need simply to go on. So she hadn't dwelt on sex, on the possibility that she had never really come to life at someone's touch; she knew she had felt pleasure, if not an ecstasy with a will of its own, an end to longing. Now, in this man's arms, she was conscious of death as she felt his heartbeat through her breast, and of a flood of serenity washing over her previous self, soothing, healing.

She had stopped thinking about the difference in their ages as one stops thinking about consequences of any kind when love begins to form its isolating circle, however worn its promise. They were spending as much time together as they possibly could, learning each other's habits, preferences, moods. Their work schedules were brutal. Terrence was mounting a drama by a new playwright with the City Theater Club's usual sparse budget and harried timetable. As the opening grew near she watched his manner, his whole being, become increasingly intense, not angry or even disengaged but stretched to a tautness that was like a long scream. She attended a rehearsal and was startled to find that there Terrence presided over recurring chaos with infinite calm, knowing his way, getting it amiably. She herself was feeling slightly frenetic; the two days a week she did *The Morning Show* were losses, throwing her off the writing schedule she had finally settled into after numerous bouts with procrastination, some of which had bordered on the suicidal. Now, on Mondays and Thursdays, she was expected to read a one- or two-minute piece, shorter than her column, neater, immediately digestible. She was also expected to get up at an ungodly hour and would therefore go to bed too early and awaken in the middle of the night, or go to bed too late and be exhausted the next day. What counted, despite the fun she was having with television—by which she meant her association with it rather than the physical fact of being on it—was her column. She had no intention of letting it get away from her.

Terrence fueled her with energy; love did. They stayed together a few nights a week and most weekends at his home in Brooklyn Heights. Beth didn't feel Georgie was in shape for a male guest as yet, nor did she feel comfortable leaving Georgie to her own devices for any extended period of time. Suzanne was there often and would certainly cover when needed, but Beth felt responsible for Georgie, perhaps more accurately the need to act responsibly where Georgie was concerned. She hadn't always done this, and while Dennis Mayo no longer held Beth or Georgie on the string of memory, the knowledge of that failure was, in Beth's mind, still acute.

She wondered if every life held one big lie, or just a thousand small ones, called into service to muddle the facts sufficiently well so that one not only escapes culpability, but actually believes in the rightness of being off the hook. The mind is a wonderful thing for deception, she knew. She was experiencing love, what she had always taken to be love and somehow always missed, by an inch here, a mile there, and still she hadn't been able to tell Terrence about her own big cover-up, the child she'd once had. She saw in him, in their coming together, the possibility of renewal.

But only if she came clean.

eighteen

That first time, on her way to meet the photographer Jack David, in the blouson linen shirt, the baggy skirt and the low-slung belt that Beth assured her could stylishly camouflage mounds of imperfection, Georgie was terrified. She could no more picture Jack David or the setting where they would work than she could imagine how her mouth and tongue would make decipherable sounds once she got there. This was, she thought, what her children must have felt, deposited at kindergarten for the first time. But no one was there to pat her backside with reassurance, to blow the kisses that would propel her through the revolving door of the building on East Fifteenth Street.

Could these be the kitchens of Mary Lee? They looked as inviting as hospital sheets. When she thought of the chocolate fudge swirl she'd gorged on, the cinnamon apple and pecan surprise that had fed her wounds, the raspberry (or blueberry, or apricot) supreme that had soothed her soul in the dead of night, it didn't seem possible they'd been concocted here; the place reeked of ammonia, the sinks were stainless steel and there were no elves in sight. No elves! She had just resolved to have a serious word with Suzanne about truth in advertising when her employer appeared.

Jack David was short. He carried his protruding belly, which Georgie could have kissed, with the ease of a man who had always been preceded by it. His beard was pointed, nearly white.

"Jack David?" she had said.

"I lopped off the 'off'," he said.

She stared at him. Jack off? "Davidoff," she said, praying for her first gold star.

She racked up stars all afternoon, pleasing Mr. David né Davidoff, except for the one time when she reached in with her finger to smooth a frosting while he was shooting. And the time she backed into the light cord and tripped, jerking it out of its socket and upending the strobe, causing Jack David to make a surprisingly agile lunge for it. He had resumed very calmly, she thought.

Now they had been on three shoots together, all for the same client, and Georgie, feeling somewhat experienced as an assistant and second to no one in her intimate knowledge of the full line of Mary Lee baked goods, offered an occasional opinion. For example, she pointed out that probably no woman in America, baking a chocolate cake in her own kitchen, would put a maraschino cherry in the middle of it.

"Ever been to the Midwest?" Jack asked.

"I'm *from* the Midwest."

"Hmm," he said. And glanced at the usually chirpy home

economist from Mary Lee who was always in attendance, her eyes bulging now, and kept the cherry. The account executive and the art director from the ad agency that had hired him nodded in relief.

The thing about Mary Lee cake mixes was that when they showed you what the finished products would look like, there was always something on them you'd want to pick off. But Georgie, having just barely hobbled onto reasonably steady ground, held her tongue.

She liked Jack. He never seemed to be probing; he was a dentist with laughing gas, painlessly extracting what was necessary so that he could place Georgie, set her down somewhere. He knew that Georgie was not living with her husband, although this could be viewed as temporary; he knew the names of her three children and what they were doing, at least to the degree that Georgie did; and he knew that this job represented the possibility of a comeback for her from a dangerously low ebb. He didn't know that she had planned to weasel out of it, showing up that first time only because of a disinclination to distress Beth and Suzanne, who had clucked over her like increasingly apprehensive hens as the day drew near, and because of a mild curiosity—to which she'd never have admitted. But then after that first time it was too late; she was sucked in, hooked; she had enjoyed herself.

At home now, in Beth's apartment, there were times when Georgie felt as if she were caught in a time warp: they were college roommates again, going off in different directions, coming back flushed, dreaming under the same roof. The feeling vanished on those nights when Beth slept out; when they snacked on celery and carrot sticks; when Georgie met Terrence for the first time and felt, to her chagrin, like the mother of a teenager who had been told the usual nothing.

Georgie found Terrence to be overwhelming: huge and bright and far too visible for her taste—an interesting thought for someone who wasn't entirely sure she still had a taste. She tried to imagine him naked, she who had slept with two men in her life and powdered and squeezed one boy child, and came up with a decidedly blurred mass of freckles and flesh. She kept working at it. She tried to imagine Jack David without his clothes on, and men on the street, but it was never quite right, her eye was excessively prudish and malfunctioned entirely when it came to conjuring genitalia. At such times she would think of Lew and his everyday body and his everyday cock and remember she was a regular person who knew of such mysteries.

When she had first moved in with Beth, Lew had called her regularly every night, intoning his concern. She would listen patiently and then instantly forget everything he said, a congregation of one. Now he called every other day, or twice a week. Talking with him, Georgie felt the way she had when her father called her at college: impatient with this voice from the past that bore no relation to her present, and just barely tolerant of its incognizance. Like her father, Lew meant well. Like her father, he lacked subtlety, nuance. This realization was not new, merely heightened, oddly enough, in his absence.

The children she carried everywhere. She had been fully prepared to reassure them of her stability, of her love for them, of there being no need for them to fly home and hover over the "accident" victim. They were to go on with their lives, they still had two parents who would work this out between them whatever way they could, but in any event would still be there for them, as always. Shawn, her baby, accepted this with what she thought was embarrassed relief, but then Shawn was at an age where everything was either embarrassing or relieving.

Melissa had cried over the telephone. Georgie could picture her sitting on the floor of her room, the door closed over the cord attached to the phone in the hall. Missy knew very well it hadn't been an accident; Georgie imagined they all knew. Missy wanted to quit school and come home, maybe enroll at NYU and live with Georgie (to watch, protect) until . . . well, maybe they'd all go back to Larchmont. Georgie was deeply touched, knowing how very much her daughter loved Tom Golden, who was there at school. "I understand about divorce, Mom. I'm not going to fall apart if that's what you decide you want," she had said, gathering her womanhood. "But I think you and Dad should go for counseling first and at least try, because a third party, someone removed from it, maybe could . . . Mom?" It was agreed that Melissa would stay at Carlisle.

The eldest, Laura, gave her mother a week to collect herself and then she flew in from San Francisco, realizing on the flight that it was she who needed time; time to get used to the being who occupied Georgie's body and was called Mother. She knocked down three Scotches in four-and-a-half hours and wobbled off the plane with a forward tilt, still reaching for the trail of clues that would reveal this woman whom she had lived with, touched and loved all these years without bothering to see her, without troubling to question. She'd had, after all, so much else with which to be occupied; she'd had herself.

It was different with Beth, and Suzanne; Laura had always been intensely curious about them, gobbling up every morsel she could coax from Georgie about their men, their work, their lives. By the time Laura was old enough to notice, they were both divorced, both successful. It wasn't that they seemed more lively than Georgie, or even more appealing. It was rather that they were doing what Laura was expected to do, eventually, just as Georgie had done what was expected of her. Beth and Suzanne, in Laura's eyes, were among the mavericks of their generation, which heightened her interest. These women were exciting; Georgie was Mother.

"Dad loves her, and Mom accepts his love as if it were one of the elements: constant, basic, beyond her control. She's never gone *toward* him; she just doesn't turn away." The moment Laura said this to Beth, that first night, she realized she knew it only in retrospect. In fact, she knew nothing about her parents' feelings in the present, which might bear no relation to what she had just described. She thought Beth knew, but her mother's old friend was not going to tell.

Beth looked radiant; far better, Laura thought, than when she'd seen her last, several months before. She was a beautiful woman, her features so perfectly sculpted that even her sadness tended to appear doll-like and thus, inconsequential: Barbie cries, Barbie pouts.

Laura spent three days in New York and then had to go back home, back to work. She left believing that her mother was out of danger in terms of another attempt on her own life; Suzanne had told her quite matter-of-factly that Georgie didn't repeat herself, which Laura recognized as true the instant she heard it. She felt, too, that in the care of Beth and Suzanne her mother would be safe; even though Georgie might slide into some underlayer of bedrock, she'd never be out of reach of their affection and attention, of their love. Was she handing her over, then? Relieving herself, as well as Shawn, Missy and even their father of responsibility, of fear? But Beth and Suzanne understood this woman, her mother; they knew her secrets. Laura was just beginning to realize Georgie had secrets, and that they may not be any of her business. This was particularly difficult to accept when Laura visited her father. Lew had always been wiry and muscular, but now he was gaunt, his skin suddenly flabby, and his eyes seemed to have sunk into deep wells, giving him a furtive, surprised look. She'd seen that look on various friends over the years, and had endured it herself, but had never expected the pain of a broken heart to be baldly etched on her father's face; parents were precluded from such emotional turmoil by virtue of their inexperience—what did they know of love? She wondered when her mother and her father had turned into these other people, strangers even to each other. Where were her parents? Had she dreamed it all? But Georgie said, as if she believed it, we're not just the past, we're still becoming; be patient with us.

And so it seemed, all these months later, that everything had been laid to rest, or at least put on hold. Georgie was still alive. She was working. She was thinner. She had lost nineteen pounds, primarily by walking instead of riding and looking instead of eating. She made a dismal attempt to exercise each morning, holding her place in Jane Fonda's book with her elbow while her legs shot up. Within minutes she'd be struggling to control a fierce desire for milk and double-chocolate-chip cookies, accustomed as she was, as a serious eater, to rewarding herself whenever she had been a good girl. Once, feeling her resolve faltering, she ate a rice cake, which caused her to look forward to abstention.

The trouble was that within a matter of weeks colleges would be setting free their charges, which meant Shawn and

Melissa would be coming home. But where was home? They both had plans for the summer: Shawn was going to Texas with two friends to work on a ranch, and Melissa was joining her roommate in Marblehead, where they were set to work in the bookstore owned by the girl's family. Still, none of this would take place until late in June; they would come home to Larchmont as they always had, because there was no other place for them to go. Georgie had no real sense of what they'd find there—she had not been to the house even once, and while she didn't think it had physically changed in all these months, she knew there must be some reflection of her absence. It struck her as peculiar that she had never worried over the care and attention her home was no longer receiving. Lew was relatively neat, and had kept on the housekeeper who came once a week. But without Georgie there to direct her—more important, without Georgie there to maintain the house at a certain level every day of the week, keeping it clean for the housekeeper, as Lew often said, she knew what to expect. By now, dust would have gathered in hidden corners, copper pots would be tarnished, the oven crusted, the wood floors starving for oil and polish, the refrigerator's odors defying detection; oh, she knew, with the certainty of a woman who had long ago convinced herself of her own necessity. And hadn't much cared until now.

She wanted to be there for her children as she had always been. She wished there was some way to suspend her new life and the old mistakes that fathered it, just for a short period of time; just long enough to play house convincingly until the kids went off again. The fact that for Shawn and Melissa the house would be merely a pit stop, a Laundromat where one could fuel up with food, hardly mattered: you either took care or you didn't. Her kids were used to a mother who did. For despite her obvious failures (and the many she tried to hide) Georgie knew she had been a good mother—a bloody good one—which was a lot more than a lot of people could say.

Also less.

nineteen

Jerry Widener, the producer of the morning news, was going to be fired; it said so in the *New York Post* and *USA Today.* The male host was going to be replaced, probably by the number one anchorman in Los Angeles *(LA Times, Variety)* or Bill Moyers *(NY Times, Wall Street Journal)* or Bernie Slotnick from Freeport, Long Island (Marvin Kitman/ *Newsday*). The network spokesperson said, "We have absolutely no plans whatever to replace anyone on the morning news; our ratings always go down in the summer."

It was hot. Terrence had rented a cottage in northwestern Connecticut, where various *New Yorker* writers were rumored to be stashed in the woods, where men played tennis in blue shorts and black socks, and no one threw catered cocktail parties.

The town "beach" was a hard patch of dirt thinly layered with sand, on loan to residents by its local owner. There were park benches, occasional patches of grass and two toilet sheds. A board was propped up against the empty lifeguard tower, listing fifteen activities that were prohibited. The lake, its velvety bottom loosing minnows wherever one walked, seemed to have been scooped out in the center of a lush forest, lined with weeping willows.

Stretched out on the dock after a long swim, Beth raised a knee and rolled back and forth on her hips to the rhythm of a very indolent "I'm Biding My Time." She felt fresh, almost new, as if the lake had purged her of the past and transformed her into a young girl again, fearless, languid, dreamy. Terrence's fingers touched hers, a reminder that the lake had had help.

Beth preferred it this way, just the two of them away for the weekend, with no particular plans. They were still so new to each other they didn't need anyone else. And while Beth was loath to admit it, when other people were around she wasn't completely relaxed; other people were liable to say embarrassing things, whether mischievously or inadvertently. She had been embarrassed at a recent dinner party when a woman had remembered her from Carlisle, although they hadn't been friends or even in the same class; the woman then plunged on to Terrence, insisting on his school, major, year. She was a bore, and Terrence decided they'd been going out too much, saying yes too often. That Beth's reaction had been mortification at this uncovering of the years that separated them was beyond his comprehension.

"Didn't you see her face?" Beth had said, "The way she looked at me? Then her husband, my God he was leering, you must have seen it!" She was staring at Terrence when suddenly she heaved a sigh. "I can't believe I'm saying this," she said. "I can't believe I'm thinking it."

She stopped saying it, but she was thinking it and he knew she was. When his latest production opened at the City Theater Club, to respectable if not rave reviews, they attended a party with the cast and an assortment of people who found their way to such celebrations like homing pigeons. An extraordinarily beautiful model, nearly his size, gushed at Terrence, her thick brows furrowed in earnestness, her nose nearly touching his. Beth liked the fact that he didn't hide his enjoyment, and that he didn't let go of her hand. But then Newton Briggs, a wizened cherub in crew cut and bow tie who delivered feature stories on the local news that centered on such questions as which direction people licked their ice-cream cones, stared at them bug-eyed.

"When did this start?" he purred. Beth watched his bow tie dance. Terrence said nothing.

"It's all the rage, you know, not to be embarrassed. Well, it makes perfect sense, doesn't it? Everyone knows men peak at seventeen and women just go on and on . . . God screwed up when it comes to screwing." He looked at Terrence, then at Beth. "I love it. I *love* it." He squeezed their shoulders as if they were bookends, caught someone's eye and skipped away.

Terrence said, "What an ass."

"Then why do I feel like Helen Trent?"

"Who?"

"There, you see? Poor old thing. Wrung her heart out over the airwaves to prove a woman could still find love after thirty-five, all for an audience of housewives and little girls home from school with a cold or measles, when it was men she should have been convincing."

"Ahh, but what about the time Opie fell in love with his teacher?" Terrence said.

"Who?"

It was difficult to let it go, this difference in their ages, although she wasn't entirely sure why. The years between them seemed to have no particular effect on their lives together. In fact they had many passions in common, a lovers' compendium of preferences—for Mamet and Miller, for pasta, Mozart, lake swimming, blueberries, for Lena Horne, Sundays, eating in. The list seemed endless and continued to grow, as it does when lovers are still discovering those things they actually learned to enjoy alone, as if in preparation for this moment when they could, by sharing them, enshrine them. They were learning to please each other; they even imagined they were unraveling each other and getting a peek inside.

He asked her about Donald, her ex-husband. He said that everyone he knew who was divorced talked about it endlessly, as if they thought if they said the secret word, the pain would disappear. But you, he told her, say nothing.

First he asked her, "What was it like being married?"

She considered for a moment. "It was like two people living together who loved each other once," she said, wondering if that was true. She was squinting at the sun, closing one eye, then the other, intrigued by the blurred colored spots.

Then he asked about Donald. She rolled over to one side and gave him her relaxed, smiling face, clear of irony, guilt or malice. "Donald is a partner at a venerable old firm on Wall Street, he is making money in barrels and rolling it home to his baronial estate in the sky—a ten-room apartment somewhere on Fifth—and no doubt diverting some of it to his other estate in Pound Ridge. Donald and Sonia, who actually looks a little bit like Sonja Henie, and God, don't ask me who that is, have what is known in some circles as everything."

"Ah, but can she skate?" Terrence said, pleased with himself. His eyes were unusually bright, his skin ruddy and freckled from the sun. She felt suddenly overwhelmed with love for him; it constricted her chest and made her feel leaden. She knew she had not felt this way in years, that it was possible she had never felt this way even though she carried the memory of it, perhaps from a dream. But she hadn't been waiting for it, hadn't expected it, not at her age. It seemed to her that it did have something to do with age, with experience of course, with weariness masquerading as pragmatism. How many old radicals could one count? How many old fools?

In the early evening they tried to have cocktails in the backyard, a huge expanse butted up against the woods, and had to give it up; gnats were on the attack and drove them indoors. They settled in the small living room because it afforded a view of the garden and an especially graceful Japanese elm.

Beth wondered about the woman who lived here, from whom Terrence had rented. She'd been able to piece together a few facts: that she was a graduate of a women's college and about three years older than Beth—mail had come from the alumni office with "Class of '58" emblazoned on it; that she was neither married nor living with a man; and that she didn't have children, who nearly always leave their mark even when they're long gone.

The house itself gave off confusing clues. There were attempts at a certain formality: wall-to-wall carpeting in the living, dining and sitting rooms, silver candle holders on the dining table, the "good" china stacked neatly in an adjacent closet, love seats, wing and club chairs covered to taut perfection, and an entire wall, floor to ceiling, of fine hardcover books from a variety of disciplines: classic works of fiction and poetry, titles on the plight of women and the black experience in

America, collections of English and French plays, tracts on sociology, anthropology, psychotherapy, economic theory, and one nod to rural Connecticut's cold winter nights, a paperback copy of *Fear of Flying.*

But the bookshelves were formed by black tin rods that fit together like pieces from a child's erector set; when you sat in the chairs, their pillows sunk into small, hard wells that only solid and repeated poundings could remove; and the slipcovers, odd prints chosen seemingly at random, could not withstand the slightest movement without coming hopelessly loose from the corners under which they'd been yanked and tucked. The carpet was thick but rippled every few feet. The windows were astonishingly clean, but would stay open only with a book propped under them; Beth had a terrible time choosing the titles for such mundane and possibly damaging work, until Terrence pointed out that among the authors whose works were hefty enough to be considered, Mailer and Friedan were the ones that could withstand the pressure.

There were questions everywhere one looked. The walls were smooth, the ceilings chipped and peeling; the front of the house had been newly shingled; the back was rotting, the silver gleamed and the pots were dirty, cookbooks took up an entire shelf in the kitchen, while frozen hors d'oeuvres filled the freezer and Dinty Moore variations lined the pantry. There were glasses of every variety, for wine, highballs, brandy and cordials, and a liquor supply cadged from Delta and Pan Am. The water didn't run if the man next door had his hose on; spiders clung to the bathtub with a fragile tenacity, as if they knew the odds.

The drive up, though, was luxurious, a voyage over curved, nearly empty roads lined with flourishing trees. Closer in, there were brooks, waterfalls, wild arrays of tiger lilies, small homes gleaming with fresh paint and carefully tended flower patches. And the house, on a high mound of land off the main road, filled them with an enormous sense of relief each time they approached it; it was of no identifiable shape, it said nothing and so demanded nothing. The air was sweet-smelling and there seemed to be enough of it. They slept in a four-poster bed, the crisp night breeze coming through a window held securely open by *Ancient Evenings.*

Beth thought of the woman whose bed and table she had used as her own, and tried to imagine her life. It was as if a proper face had to be presented to the world, as if the unpleasantness of emptiness, of cries in the night—the rotten truth—had to be kept under wraps so as not to despoil the landscape. She was jumping to conclusions, perhaps, but it didn't seem so. She felt an affinity for this woman, who just managed to carve out for herself a piece of a life, gently knocking at the edges of other people's well-being, frozen h'ors d'oeuvres in hand. She couldn't help but know this, it seeped into her woman's consciousness each time she entered the house. She knew her as the embodiment of her own fears. Beth had been lucky, that was all: she and Donald had found each other at college and had stayed married long enough, a decade, to care about the rest of each other's lives. They had slid away from each other without rancor; childless, guiltless. And Beth had been happy for him when he married Sonia—who had she been seeing at the time? She couldn't remember, nor did it matter; the point was that life went on, that a step to the left or a feint to the right had made it possible for her to retain her membership in this world, to form sexual, emotional, intellectual bonds, to be connected.

She had told Donald she loved him, all those years ago. And told herself in the years that followed that she was a child then, what could she have known of love? Until it occurred to her that she was still hazy on the subject, perhaps because she'd had so little practice. There was almost always someone, nibbling at the edge of her life or squarely in it; she had cared for each of them, in varying degrees. That it wasn't "love" disturbed her less and less as the years went by—her work was fulfilling and demanding, so much so that companionship and good sex were like gleaming pennies one stumbled on often enough to ease the rumblings of one's heart.

Now here she was with her red giant, dizzy with love. Not so dizzy that she imagined herself being brought home to Terrence's father as the "girl" of his dreams. What she had here was temporary, she knew that. He loved her, but at some point he'd remember that he wanted children; at some point he'd start to think seriously about the fact that when he was forty-seven—her age now, but for him, for any man, it had a younger ring—she'd be over sixty. She meant to enjoy every moment of it without deluding herself, expecting absolutely nothing.

She was old enough to know better.

twenty

Georgie was working constantly now, not only with Jack David, but on her own. She actually had a business going, although she didn't yet think of it as such—perhaps because it began by chance. When a dinner party Beth had planned was about to be derailed because she found herself having to be on the road directly before it, Georgie jumped in and prepared the meal for her. All that was required was for Beth's guests to swoon over Georgie's delectable artichoke bottoms with foie gras, chicken Kiev, semolina gnocchi, *endives braisées* and apricot ice, and to declare themselves in dire need of such service, and Georgie's business was born.

Before she knew it, she was a small rage. She'd even been chauffeured to a real estate mogul's "farm" in the Hamptons in a brown Mercedes limousine the length and breadth of an aircraft carrier, her bulging grocery bags stashed in the trunk,

Georgie nestled in the back sipping orange juice from a crystal glass, shouting cheery small talk to the driver. If one person had her, someone else had to, which got her out of the steamy city and into cool country houses on weekends, there to be treated not as "help," but as a guest with a particular skill. She was exhilarated even when she was dog tired, and as light on her feet as she'd been in years. Pounds, ripples, even small tires were gradually falling off her frame, uncovering not exactly her old self but a recognizable facsimile. When people inquired as to what wondrous diet she had discovered, she would attempt to explain that once food became her work it no longer held the same appeal; under the circumstances it didn't seem necessary to add that there were even occasions when the mere sight of food made her nauseated.

This particular Friday, her stomach steady, Georgie was preparing cold beef *en daube* with horseradish cream, and rice salad, which would be served with double consommé of chicken and a cold orange soufflé at a dinner for ten the following evening in Easthampton. She had deliberately chosen a menu that would, for the most part, keep overnight: she was determined to take her place around the pool with all the other lollers who were houseguests, all those captains of industry and their skinny wives and their bronze kids and their charming, interesting, single and occasionally heterosexual friends.

"What you need to do," Jack had said, "is run this like a business."

"I am. I do. I make a profit," Georgie said defensively.

Jack snorted. "You're in demand, Georgie, you're supposed to capitalize on that. So what do you do? You schlepp shopping bags to Southampton or Quogue and because they give you guest privileges and a room done in wicker you think it's not nice to make money."

"Easthampton. It's Easthampton this weekend," she corrected him. And as it turned out it wasn't wicker, it was rattan, everywhere she looked: the headboard, the trunk at the base of the bed, the quaint little desk and the frames of two incredibly plump chairs. A vivid handmade quilt lay gaily, casually, on the bed. The entire fifteen-room, turn-of-the-century house was gay and casual, as were the guests, stripped down to their bathing suits and their Rolexes, lying in woven contour chaises nestled between vast pots of geraniums at the edge of a sparkling, free-form unused pool. It was all so country; Georgie should have felt right at home.

Nan Levin, her hostess (client) welcomed her with open arms. Georgie was, after all, on intimate terms with Elizabeth Emerson and Terrence O'Neil, not to mention who *their* friends were, and Nan had been the first to import her eastward.

Georgie was used to money; her father had made a lot of it, so had Lew. But something of the Midwest still clung to her. She was not totally at ease with these New York City women, whose polished exteriors she imagined to be their birthright. She was not exactly overwhelmed, merely a visitor from another country where she, too, could be counted among the elite; it was the foreign tongue, the odd customs, that were off-putting.

And so she sat still for all the questions put to her with practiced dispatch by Nan Levin, such as what schools had her children attended and what schools were they now attending and what schools had she attended and what did her husband do and how long had she been separated and where did she get that marvelous caftan and what had she served up for Lally and Will in Southampton and who was there and how was that incredible Beth whose column on condoms and the sexual responsibility of males she had Xeroxed and given to all three of her daughters who were eleven, thirteen and fifteen and before Georgie knew it she had even answered how old is she really?

Of course she didn't ask any of her own questions, such as why was Mickey Levin always stoned. And how (why) did the Weirs get their six-year-old to bow and offer his little hand forcefully when introduced. And who was or had been sleeping with whom here because that much was clear: sharing was permitted. Or perhaps Georgie had a rube's ear for nuance in this strange land, where her entrée was her entré.

"Doesn't this strike you as peculiar?" she had protested nervously to Jack before her first weekend foray.

"Revolutionary, I'd say," Jack said.

"Postrevolutionary," Georgie said. "Now the cook eats with the cookees. Isn't that mixing the downstairs with the upstairs?"

"You're as upstairs as any of them; you're just more accomplished at the art of cooking, for which you are being paid. And you are at least equally accomplished at the art of sociability, for which you are being invited. I even have a slogan for you: 'Entrée-Nous.' "

She loved it, but told Suzanne, who had happily offered her skills, to hold off on designing the cards and the stationery because she wanted to think about it. The truth was she was scared to operate on the assumption that what she was doing could not be blown away at any moment, even by a light wind. Why couldn't it? She hadn't had a job in twenty-five years, much less a profession; it was just that Beth was dropping her name everywhere, as Jack was in his world, and Dale and Suzanne in theirs, and after the initial few who would bite—for reasons having nothing to do with Georgie but out of their desire to please whoever mentioned her—she'd be using that stationery for grocery lists and letters to the kids.

On the other hand, she had to admit her dinners were successful; they were, in fact, incredibly good. Deep down, Georgie was thrilled and relieved to find that she had an operable skill, a talent that was economically viable, although initially it depressed her that it was merely an outgrowth of her previous life, that after all these years, she was still cooking. By the time she had prepared her third meal for strangers, and received her third check, it was clear to her that what she was doing was unlike anything she had done before, and her spirits soared.

Sitting by the pool now, Georgie wanted to swim, but she'd forgotten her hair dryer, and there was David Metzger beside her, Dr. David Metzger, with tinted aviator glasses and a wonderful thatch of gray hair. Besides, what if the pool had never been used, what if it contained dangerous chemicals that made it appear as pure as bottled water and wasn't meant to be swum in?

It occurred to her that if Dr. David had been a woman, he'd have dyed his hair by now. Every part of him was, Georgie could see, pampered to perfection, right down to his manicured toes. She imagined his masseur, his game of raquetball, his one good after-dinner cigar. The man had to be living on skinless chicken, brown rice and steamed vegetables to look that good; only his taste buds had shriveled. He was, she figured, fifty or fifty-two, had been married once, briefly, and had neither children nor pets that might wrinkle a bed or pee importunely. Dr. David was sleek, and yet not off-putting. He probably liked his mother.

"I'm simply saying," he was saying, "that second marriages

have no greater chance of succeeding than first marriages; to imagine that age and wisdom make for better choices is not necessarily the way things turn out. Mostly, people continue to make the same mistakes. It's just that they're more practiced at self-delusion."

"Everybody doesn't make the same mistakes," Nan Levin said, with a hint of petulance.

"You're taking this personally, Nan—I'm not talking about you and Mickey, or Karen and Tom," he said, nodding in the Weir's direction. "But you know the numbers, they're printed regularly and offered up like some kind of national barometer of our failings. The percentages may be exaggerated but the nub is true enough—the divorce rate is high, even for second marriages."

"Is that what you tell your patients when they're considering another plunge?" the thrice-married Karen Golden asked.

"No, no. He tells them to go for it, so they'll keep having to come back to him," Mickey Levin said, laughing.

"Are you a psychiatrist?" Georgie asked.

Dr. David nodded, then turned to her as if remembering she was there. "Got a problem?"

"Christ, he's shilling again," Mickey said, causing David Metzger embarrassment at his own flippant remark, she thought, as well as Mickey's, which caused Georgie to forgive him for being perfect, which of course he wasn't. She knew that, it was just that Georgie hadn't been attracted to a man in so long she thought she had already lived that part of her life and was doomed to live out the rest of her statistically probable eighty-plus years remembering it. And so she might be going just a slight bit overboard, imagining, for example, what it would be like to have his child and name it Sasha.

Georgie was suddenly alert to an aroma that never failed to arouse in her a reminder that she had missed The Sixties; that when asked about that era by her children she could only recount it from the curious vantage point of a young outsider, which made her feel vaguely guilty. She had graduated well before the time when flower children and hippies began pushing the envelope of civil disorder on campuses and in the streets; well before a male student would be caught dead in a pony tail. Georgie wasn't taken much by these nodding waifs, who seemed, despite their rhetoric, to be almost exclusively self-indulgent. But when it counted, as when the civil rights movement gathered momentum and she could have joined, could have marched, protested—where was she? Paying lip service only, her personal rebellion with Dennis Mayo all the action she could handle. More than she could handle. So in all those years, those hopeful, violent, naïve, permissive years, Georgie hadn't smoked pot, taunted the cops, whipped herself into a sexual frenzy, worn peace symbols, heaved bags of excrement, pressed flowers into the hands of the forgiven or taken what could be considered a genuine stand—where something was at risk—on anything. After Dennis, her one stab at fearlessness, she had crawled back home, married Lew and fell into step in the life she had been taught to embrace. She understood that she hadn't been raised a Spock baby, the kind who could call her father a capitalist pig and then get the keys to the car; that in her field of reference, fuck-yous would not have elicited parental understanding and that sociological phenomenom, the adolescent family: If you're going to smoke a joint, son, we'd rather you did it at home, with us. What she couldn't quite forgive herself for was her rush to judgment, her unquestioning alignment with the grown-ups, as if the need to prove she was one of them, taking her rightful place, overrode the possibility of independent thought. When Georgie finally grasped the tragedy of Vietnam it was at the center of a national malaise, a hot red ball that was threatening to melt the country's heart; that it took her so long caused her a profound shame she had admitted to no one, ever. The smell of marijuana always brought it back.

Georgie thought she had sniffed out the familiar, thickly sweet odor surreptitiously, just as in similar circumstances with her kids she thought she performed thorough air checks with absolutely convincing nonchalance, but it was true in neither case. Mickey Levin was tilting a joint in her direction, and Georgie shook her head no in what she hoped would appear as a nonjudgmental, even casual gesture—as if she was offered marijuana all the time and just didn't happen to feel like it at this particular moment. She could feel David Metzger watching her.

"Egad, a grown-up," he said, quietly, only for Georgie's ears. They smiled at each other. She sat back in her chair, her eyes closed, still smiling. Thinking, my God he's attracted to me, is that possible? But I'm attracted to him, why shouldn't he be attracted to me? Because he isn't, you idiot, he's just being nice, polite to the worker bee, that's it, isn't it, of course that's it, oh shit why am I even thinking about this? I don't want to think about this, it's completely dumb.

"You're very attractive," he said to the closed eyes, the widening smile. "For a caterer."

Had he said that? He hadn't said that, not that last part. Georgie stole a look at the face he was presenting; it was gentle, expectant, not a face that had qualified a compliment with a snide remark. That was Georgie's work, her way of diffusing her own complacency all those years when obesity could be forgiven or even disowned by a kind remark: You look wonderful, Georgie (for a fat lady); love that dress (because it covers you). She relied on her own wisecracks, rarely spoken aloud but loud enough inside her head, to soften the effect of what she was sure people were really thinking.

"Swim with me," Dr. David commanded.

"Is it permitted?" Georgie said, making him laugh, thinking about her dryer and her body under the marvelous caftan. She still couldn't get used to her thinner self; irrationally, it caused her to feel exposed, as if the layers of fat had been not only debasing but protective. She was proud of her new body yet afraid to show it off; she had been out of the fray for so long.

David Metzger, knowing none of this, was unzipping her caftan and helping her out of it and Georgie, having quickly realized that all eyes were not upon her, turned crimson with embarrassment—which David took as an endearing blush at his own frank admiration of her wonderfully soft, zaftig body. David dove into the pool, Georgie climbed.

She hadn't realized how small his bathing suit was, how small *he* was from waist to thigh. He had the smallest ass she'd ever seen on a man; she thought if they made love she'd kill him—but wait, that was the old Georgie, surely not this lithe, comparatively graceful variety. She was thinking about making love, about sex most specifically, as if it hadn't occurred to her in years. Perhaps it hadn't, as a conscious thought. She had reacted when Lew touched her, but couldn't remember ever seeking him out. Now Georgie the ex-housewife was sneaking looks through the water at David Metzger's penis, which bulged like a pair of thick, curled-up socks. Her nipples hurt, which meant they looked terrific, quivering near the water line.

She felt suddenly aware of all parts of her; her toes were curling involuntarily, water was lapping around her cunt, she who had forgotten she had one and in any event always referred to it as "down there." Like other fifties girls, she had trouble saying certain words she had once hunted for and dog-eared in books, most notably fuck and cunt. Why, Georgie had women friends who were only five or six years younger and easily tossed off cocks and pricks and cunts like you would shits and damns; she always expected them to look self-conscious, or to quickly lower their voices, as if, in passion, the unmentionable had slipped out, but of course this never happened. How could those few years change an entire culture? she often wondered, for she believed they had. David Metzger was from her world. She liked that.

After dinner, a notable success, David and Georgie went walking to the ocean, which was a few blocks of imposing homes away. As they left, there was a ripple of attention paid, for here might be a first: the two single people on hand actually seemed able to stand each other's company, when nothing whatever had been planned or plotted. It was only after they left that bets were taken on how far they would go. Georgie was oblivious. She had taken great pains with her appearance, like a teenager prepping for an important date, any date, feeling slightly ridiculous and yet remembering exactly how to do it, exactly how it felt. It was all-consuming, and while some thinking part of her managed to wonder if women were forever doomed to this, the answer was obliterated by the concentration required to apply eye liner and shadow, then smudge and remove most of it.

Why was David Metzger bringing back all these memories? She couldn't imagine, unless the romantic feelings he stirred within her had just naturally triggered thoughts of that time in her life when romance was within her sensory knowledge. It was all so long ago, tucked away with pressed flowers gone chalky, and faded photos of those strangers, her other selves. It would never have occurred to her that an emotional resurrection was conceivable, for that was how she thought of her feelings at this moment, as if some part of her had been reborn. Or perhaps the capacity for romantic love, for falling in love, never leaves us; perhaps, for sheer survival, we cover it over as one lowers the shade to a blinding sun in the heat of the day.

David held her hand as they walked along the water's edge. His touch seemed quite natural and so she was barely conscious of it; even their rhythm as they walked was similar. He told her about his marriage some years ago to a beautiful girl he'd barely known, of her three perpetually yipping Yorkshire terriers and her insistence they all sleep together, of attempting to make love in the midst of these jealous, venomous creatures, all the while imagining where they might sink their teeth if they got the chance; well, he'd been ripe for it, his father had died suddenly at the age of sixty-one and his son the happy bachelor, recognizing that he too would one day die, set out to find himself a wife and make a family. Motivated primarily by fear, he had quite classically latched on to the first pretty face that came along and decided to love her, to plant in her the seeds of his immortality. What he reaped were three willful, pointy-nosed beasts and a warped view of conjugal bliss. Well yes, he admitted, he had exaggerated. But not much. Did Georgie have any idea what it was like to open your eyes in the morning and find, within an inch of them, another pair of eyes set in a hairy face?

Georgie heard the sound of her own laughter and delighted

in it, as if it was a lost jewel miraculously recovered in the sand. When David Metzger finally reached for her she was pleased; when he held her close she thought, oh yes, I know about this. And when, later, they made love in his room she thought she didn't know much about this at all, he was touching her, exciting her, but her mind wouldn't shut down, how had she gotten into this so quickly, they barely knew each other was what her mind said, but what archaic thinking, it felt right, didn't it feel right her mind said, it felt incredible, it was amazing how she could keep thinking oh God wasn't she supposed to ask something about sexual history about the possible presence of deadly bacteria it's gotten so complicated she thought and finally stopped thinking and came.

She regretted it within minutes, when she was thinking again. It was not uncomfortable nestled against David's shoulder, his arm holding her there; it was impersonal. She had experienced sex with so few men she felt like an anachronism, a fifties girl for whom time had stopped, stuck in the groove of a Johnny Mathis ballad. Lying next to a stranger because he looked good and had made her laugh and had wanted her.

Hungry for love.

twenty-one

Suzanne had not heard from Neal in weeks, not since her visit.

Or perhaps that wasn't entirely true. He hadn't written, but then he never wrote: to Neal, writing was on a par with the digging of root canals; his phone was a shrine. But there were times when Suzanne's phone rang and she didn't answer it, because it seemed to her to be the particular day or the exact moment that Neal would choose to call. She thought she knew such things about him, and yet she knew it was possible he hadn't called at all. Since her household was, according to Daniel and Annie, the only one in America that still didn't have an answering machine, and she was flat out of intuition, she could only guess.

It was not difficult, not answering what might be Neal's calls. Her life, her daily existence, did not change without him; Neal had never truly been "in" her life to speak of, save for those three months they had lived together. It was the constancy of her daydreams, the pathetic certainty he could cause to flood through her with that flimsiest of gifts, his promise; these were the things it was hard to let go of. She had carried him around within her, feeding on his adoration not only for nourishment, but for legitimacy. She knew she had to stop.

She was grateful to Paul Salazar, whose gallery would be featuring a group of her latest paintings, along with the work of two other artists, beginning this week. It didn't matter that she looked at that body of her work and recognized nothing, remembered nothing of the wild woman who had somehow committed it to canvas. Dale saw a finely honed eye, even an enduring grace there amidst the havoc; Suzanne saw only relief. What counted was that that thing roiling inside her had been exorcised: Neal.

"I'll never be able to paint that way again," she had said to Dale, apologetic, as if she'd caused him to mislead Salazar, as if she'd duped him.

"Of course you will. Better, probably, but you will." Dale said this thoughtfully, as always. Did he know what had propelled this frenzy of "art"? She thought he probably did. Dale always said she needed to free herself, but never said of what. Pain took care of it though, stripping one to the bone, no discretion whatever. It was horrifying at first but then, in some curiously clear-eyed way, edifying. She considered reinventing herself altogether, but it was too late and too soon. First she had to act upon what she finally knew; as for her new self, it was already forming out of scar tissue, illumination, shards of hope and other assorted brick-a-brac available at such a point in one's life.

The night before the opening of the show she'd gone to the

Salazar Gallery to see how her work was to be displayed, and met the other artists with whom the space would be shared. One was a woman in her early thirties with long curly orange hair and black-beetle eyebrows and two boys in tow, each with the bland, bony look of royalty as portrayed in Polo ads. The second artist, a man, was even younger, probably twenty-eight or so, and done up in stark playclothes calculated to exude struggle. Suzanne felt an immediate and consuming estrangement. It seemed to her that these people belonged not only to another era, but to another sensibility entirely. She'd worked with varieties of their counterparts in the agency business for years, boppers with astonishing egos, with flash and flimflam and occasional brilliance, but operating within a framework she understood. In this arena, this major industry known as the world of art, she figured the flair for mendacity and the lust for fame and fortune were also thriving; beyond that she knew nothing, other than having observed that one wasn't expected to bother with the charade of fraternizing with the enemy. Or perhaps it was just that the two young artists didn't know what to make of her either, Carol Career in her Serious Suit, moonlighting on their turf.

But Salazar had known. While Suzanne's work seemed, at first glance, to bear no relation whatever to the rest of the show, she began slowly to sense, then to see, what he must have seen. All of the work was abstract, but where theirs was severely minimalist hers appeared unrestrained, it would even seem that where they had exercised control she had run completely amok. Much to her surprise, she knew now she had not; that she had, in fact, retained at least viscerally a clear place of departure and destination. She had pressed out farther than they, with varying degrees of success to be sure; somehow, all three benefited by comparison, the whole providing the perfect setting for each of its parts.

Late in the evening she called Neal. It seemed terribly important to do this before the showing the next night; not that she expected to be unalterably affected by the public hanging of these pictures. Rather, she needed a marker. This would be the moment in time when, crouched at the ready, she'd begin to get on with her life. Calling Neal and breaking it off, whatever "it" actually still was, she equated with firing the starter gun.

He wasn't home. Suzanne vowed to keep calling even if it took half the night, because she was afraid that if she didn't make this connection at this particular time, she'd lose her will, her resolve; thought in fact that if she had to rev herself up again, her heart would give out. But she wasn't revved up; she had absorbed the truth slowly and now it was part of her. She learned this the next morning, when she awoke remembering she hadn't reached Neal and why she must; he itched, like a sweater over a sunburn.

But it was a day for other things, for marking time until the night with anticipatory flutters, small hopes and grand pleas, because this was to be the premiere of her show at Salazar's gallery. It was slated as the usual wine-and-cheese offering, attended by trendy friends of the artists and friends of their friends, a critic or two, a gang of gallery hoppers who moussed themselves up and made the downtown scene and presumably, hopefully, perhaps incidentally, the rare prospective buyer.

It didn't disappoint. The room pulsed with a sea of bobbing heads that seemed unrestrained by necks, able to turn full circle so as not to miss a face, an outfit, the art merely a backdrop for this scene of their lives. One couldn't move, couldn't navigate a path through this gaudy glut without the aid of a friendly hand attached to a strong, insistent arm. As Dale was providing such acceleration for Beth, she caught a glimpse of Suzanne, looking radiant, expectant—but Dale had no intention of letting go until he got her to the far end of the room, where, at a certain spot, he pressed her arms to her sides and turned her around.

She looked from painting to painting as if they might be taken away if she didn't hurry. Then she stepped back and studied each one carefully. When she finished she turned to Dale, who read the question in her wide eyes: How do you know a person all your life and not know this? Overwhelmed, she had begun to cry; Dale held her, and so he felt the laughter when it came up through her ribcage even before he heard it.

Soon Georgie joined them, flushed with excitement, a fellow she introduced as David Metzger at her side. Georgie was concentrating on David, on herself with David and how that felt. This was, she realized, the first time she'd actually gone somewhere in the company of any man other than Lew. She had seen David once since their meeting in the Hamptons, but they had stayed in, enjoying the sumptuous dinner Georgie had insisted on preparing. David had guessed she was uneasy about venturing out, hesitant about making this new life of hers official when she hadn't any idea, really, of what it would be like to be let loose in the world. He was right, but now she was out there and felt, after a tentative start, that she had the hang of it again; it was just like riding a bicycle. Even David Metzger's suddenly obvious enjoyment of his own attractiveness, underscored in a setting so bursting with possibility, did not throw Georgie, it only caused her to wobble a bit. Every woman in New York seemed to know David; either he had dated them and they continued to be his dear friends, or they were determined to be next on his list. Mr. Eligibility! And yet here *she* was, not yet severed from her previous and only lifetime either legally or emotionally, a poor candidate for indignant lover.

Georgie turned away from a particularly oozing assault on her senses called Myrna, who knew David when he had the house in Bridgehampton, the little red one right across from the potato field? And suddenly she was face-to-face with Suzanne: four canvases that didn't so much bespeak a life as defy it. Georgie gaped. Had she been blind to her old friend's essential being, or had some new seed been sown when her back was turned? For there, splashed all over the wall, overtaking the vision of a needy heroine consumed by her womanhood as if possessed, was an unmistakable lucidity that was so sharp it nearly hurt one's eyes.

Beth was at her elbow. "I think I saw Neal."

"Oh, shit," Georgie said. So much for revelations.

Within an hour the room had miraculously emptied, as if an alarm had been sounded for prisoners to be returned to their cells. Dale had rounded up Beth, Georgie and David, and herded them off to the special dinner he'd planned in Suzanne's honor at an Italian place he swore was an offshoot of heaven. Suzanne was nowhere to be seen, but Dale moved them along unfazed.

When they arrived, Terrence, who had had to work late, rose to greet them from their table in a back corner. Georgie saw Beth beam at the sight of him, and reflexively squeezed David's arm as if flushed herself with delight. Snapping out of it as one does from rhapsodic rubbish, she thought how easy it was for a woman to believe she had what she wanted. All it required was need.

At the gallery's center, Suzanne stood transfixed. The fact that Neal was there, waiting, that he had come to surprise her, that of course he loved her and wouldn't miss this moment in her life, all of this streamed through her at once, automatically, predictably, and she let it play itself out, a movie of her own pathology.

"Hi," Neal said, softly. He walked to her and put his arms around her. "I love you," he said. The way he always said it. As if the words were sacred. Suzanne felt her legs weaken, her lungs constrict. She pulled back from him although his arms still held her, and began punching at his shoulder, gently at first, as if to say "I am helpless in your arms, but I must at least make this attempt to prevail, humor me," and then she was punching harder, the only sound the monotonous, muted thump of the flat of her fist against his suit, shirt, skin.

He didn't move. His brows were pressed downward, his eyes squinting as if to stave off the blows; this was, she thought, how he imagined pain would look. She couldn't stop, until she saw the recognition in his face that she was finally letting go. He released her and she walked away quickly, hearing only her footsteps, leaving him standing in a puddle of his own relief.

In the cab on the way to the restaurant where a dinner was being held in her honor, Suzanne thought about food. She was starving.

twenty-two

It began when Georgie found out that Lew was seeing someone, an actual woman, with a name. Libby.

Melissa told her. She said, by way of description, however useless, that Libby was very nice. Under fire she surrendered such operative facts as Libby's size (small), her hair (blonde) and her real hair (brown). It seemed she was a physical therapist (strong) who had been divorced for almost a year, had a son in college and still lived in Larchmont.

"You're not upset, are you, Mom?" Melissa said.

"Of course not."

"I didn't think you'd be upset, or I'd never have told you. I mean, I guess I thought you knew. Mom?"

"Honey, will you stop? I am absolutely not upset."

And she wasn't; not exactly. Not at first. Then things with David Metzger took a complicated turn; she wasn't even sure how it happened, but suddenly she was on the defensive, assuring David *she* wasn't serious, either. Of course, this was true, she wasn't, but only because it was too soon; she knew she *could* be serious but these things took time. David Metzger, on the other hand, would never be serious. He and Georgie had traded amended life stories and some well-chosen secrets, but in his mind they were on the road to absolutely nowhere, unless you counted better sex as an actual destination.

"Well, what's wrong with that?" Georgie asked herself and told herself. And so David saw her and, as an unhampered man in a free country, whenever he felt like it he saw others. Georgie of course could have done the same, but she had no one to do it with; it was a free country but all was not equal.

Still, it was just a matter of adjusting, she was sure. Dating made her feel like she'd been in the pen since the fifties and was suddenly let loose in a world where kissing on the third date and petting above the waist and over the clothes first were quaint historical footnotes. It had nothing to do with being unaware of all those sexual fantasies come true that passed for real life since the late sixties. What it had to do with was being married for over twenty years; with being resolved, resigned, replete. Even, perhaps, repressed.

"Don't tell me this is breaking your heart; this is not breaking your heart," she told herself. "You enjoy being with David, it is pleasant and convenient and, let us not forget, for the moment the only game in town; nor do you pine for him in his absence." It was an honest assessment, and she might even have eked out some tolerance for David Metzger's personal credo, which she privately referred to as Trivial Pursuit, if it hadn't been for that fateful dinner she made for Terrence and Beth, with David acting as host.

Georgie had to admit she enjoyed being part of a couple. She liked David taking the coats, fixing the drinks and generating conversation while she toiled happily in the kitchen. Beth was spending so much of her time at Terrence's place it was almost as if the apartment was really Georgie's—Terrence and Beth came to the door together and David and Georgie were there to greet them. She reminded herself this was just playacting, but enjoyed it anyway. And the dinner, if she said so herself, was superb.

Beth was in the kitchen helping with dessert and coffee when it happened. They didn't know it at the time, but the moment they returned to the living room they each recognized the unease of the men. Terrence in fact looked stricken, while David's skin seemed to have gone slack. Beth's head was raised, as if she was listening for something, but Georgie didn't want to hear. They managed to get through the Charlotte Basque, a wonderful almond custard with chocolate, and even a sip or two of brandy, before David pleaded a litany of flu symptoms, each of which he appeared to have, and awkwardly got away.

They sat for a moment in silence, then Beth said, "Spill it."

Terrence looked miserably at Georgie.

"You think she doesn't know?" Beth said gently, suddenly knowing herself.

"He made a pass at me," Terrence said, shrugging, embarrassed.

"I *knew* it," Georgie said. And it seemed to her that she probably had, she must have. But it was one of those things you knew only when you heard it, that on the very instant of hearing you knew it was true: Jack Kennedy ran around, Father never really loved Mother, Hemingway wore dresses as a child. Of course!

Within twenty-four hours a distraught, horribly debased

David Metzger was at her door, come to reassure her that he was not actively bisexual despite whatever insanity had overcome him the night before, that he'd had only two experiences with men in his life, both over twenty years ago, that he had undergone the AIDS test anyway, just as an extra precaution, and come up negative, that she was not to worry, he would never, never have put her, or anyone, at risk, he was a goddamn *Doc*tor for God's sake . . . at which point Georgie, grateful and enormously moved, tried to reach for him, but he would not be comforted and ran out.

Three weeks later Lew found himself sitting alone in a restaurant in Manhattan for twenty minutes, until the new Georgie, thin with anticipation, came toward him. He stood to greet her with the kind of kiss he used to give her mother; on the other hand, his eyes shone with suitable awe at her transformation.

"You look wonderful, Georgie," Lew said. He smiled, and Georgie thought she saw his lip quiver.

"You look wonderful too," she said, surprising him. Now that she looked, he did. He had apparently gained back all the weight she'd been told he had lost; there weren't black hollows under his eyes either. She recognized his suit but the glasses were new, smoke-colored wire frames with a hint of gray in the lenses, resting lightly where horn-rims had once dug a permanent dent. His tie was new; it was a paisley with too much red in it, the sort she never bought.

With their waiter hovering, Lew asked her if she'd like something to drink and she would, she'd like a very dry vodka martini on the rocks with an olive, as the man well knew after twenty-two years. But hadn't she changed? "I'll have a Kir," Georgie said.

"And a very dry vodka martini, rocks, olive, for me," Lew said. He watched the waiter go, then shifted his eyes back to Georgie. "Well," he said, nervous, sweet, "it's very nice to see you."

There was an awkward silence. *This is a date,* she thought, *we're having a date!* "Seen any good movies lately?"

Lew laughed. "Georgie," he said.

She smiled.

"It really *is* nice to see you."

She reached for his hand and placed hers on top of it. He stared at the small pile she'd made the way a considerate child stares at lumps in his cereal. She took her hand back as if she needed it, for emphasis, or an itch, and thought how pleased she was that he had his pride.

"Can you believe the summer's over?" Georgie said, having the pace right now. "Before you know it, the kids will be home for Thanksgiving."

"I envy Shawn," Lew said. "Can you imagine . . . *my* father . . . ever letting me work . . . on a *ranch*?" Every phrase was milked for incredulity.

Georgie nodded, understanding completely this son's patriarchal history, exuding empathy; nothing had to be explained to her, the wife.

"Melissa sounds in great shape, have you talked to her?" Lew said, breaking the spell. "Oh, of course you have," he answered for her. "I wonder if it's still on with Tom, she doesn't tell me that stuff."

"It is," Georgie said.

"Ahh," Lew said, looking at her shoulder.

"And you're not happy about it."

"What are you talking about?" Lew said, his attention snapped.

"I'm talking about Tom Golden, Jewish Tom Golden," Georgie said, hearing the words fly perversely from her lips; habit.

Lew exhaled his anger, shook his head. "Have you ever heard me say anything like that, ever?"

"I didn't have to," Georgie said, trapped by what she knew. But why did she have to say it?

What was worse, Lew didn't argue. He glared at her, but then some new attitude traveled down his face; she watched it smooth out his rage, until his look was almost blissful.

Momentarily thrown by this, she decided that sex with Libby must be good—she knew the signs. In fact, there were signs of this woman all over him; he was, as she knew, the sort of man to be taken in hand.

The waiter reappeared, recited the specials, and left their menus. Hiding behind hers, Georgie resolved to behave like a sweetheart, not a wife (fighting fire with fire) but being a wife, to retain her rights. Tall order.

Lew ordered beef, as always. And Georgie, who had always done the same, chose fish. She saw this as another symbol of her changed self, a clanging clue that her husband would not fail to note.

Husband?

She hadn't thought that word in months.

So what? She was thinking it now and now was what counted.

"How's work coming along?" Lew asked.

"Really well. The free-lance part, with Jack David, is kind of sporadic, but now with the catering working out so well it's a good balance. The truth is, I can hardly believe any of this is happening, Lew, you know? It's a tremendous feeling."

"You always were an incredible cook," Lew said, beaming at her.

"I liked cooking for my family," Georgie said, beaming back.

"I know you did."

They held their breaths.

"Georgie," Lew began.

"No," she said, "let me." And struggled to find the words she thought she knew. "I know I put you through a terrible time when I, you know when I . . ."

"Georgie, that's over, it's past."

"I know, but it happened, I can't erase it. I look back and I try to remember what was going on in my head but it's elusive, kind of like retracing your steps when you were drunk. There I was with a wonderful husband and family, a beautiful home, a fine life . . ."

"No."

She looked at him, startled. "No?"

"No. You weren't happy. *We* weren't happy. I don't say that's the reason exactly, God knows millions of people aren't happy at any given time and they just go on. It's what we used to call your typical American family. The thing is, you were never typical."

"Were you?"

"Sure," Lew said comfortably. "Sure I was. Or maybe I looked at things in what I thought was the typical way. I met a girl, I fell in love with her, I married her, and years later I was still reeling from my great good fortune. I'd pull up in front of the house, you know, a hundred times, a thousand times, and still be amazed: *my* house, *my* wife, *my* kids. I never thought it would happen, you see, I never thought I'd be able to pull that off. I was so goddamn grateful, Georgie. I thought you knew that."

She did know it, of course she did, she had played it for all it was worth. And had expected to play it *now.* But where is your head, Georgie! He's in the first bloom of infatuation with someone else, flexing his muscles . . . okay, then he'll want different terms, the missionary position for life, with me the horse, him the rider. She thought, I can live with that.

"Do you think it was so different for me?" Georgie said. "Do you think I wasn't grateful? Oh Lew, twenty-two years is a long time, things happen to people, they go through stages and . . ."

"Georgie," he said without inflection, "redecorating is not a stage. We ended up the way we started out: I loved you, you didn't love me."

She smiled broadly at the waiter, who had arrived, providentially, at that moment. He distributed the plates and she busied herself, as Lew did. She thought, now we're a married couple again, dining in silence. Only this time, I am the one with something to say, and no words to say it. Lew took a bite of tenderloin with Béarnaise sauce, and put his fork down.

"How is the sole?" he asked.

Georgie swallowed a tasteless morsel. "Fine, really good," she said. She dug into her braised celery hearts, thinking what a perfect meal this was for anyone who had to gum their food. Lew offered a juicy piece of tenderloin.

"No, no really," Georgie said.

"Georgie, take it," Lew said, dropping it on her plate. She ate around it with extreme patience and finally devoured it.

"More?" he asked.

She shook her head no. He didn't insist. Where had he gone? Why couldn't she find him? It suddenly occurred to her that Libby was more of an adversary than she'd ever dreamed. She girded herself, and spoke softly.

"Tell me about her."

"Her? Libby? She's very nice."

"Nice?" Georgie said.

He started to smile. "I don't know what to say," he said.

"I don't mind talking about her," Georgie said, magnanimous, encouraging.

"I guess I do." His voice was flat.

Georgie looked at him, then stabbed a piece of fish. "Melissa's upset," she heard herself say.

"She'll get over it," Lew said.

Melissa's up*set?* "How very cavalier of you," she said.

"No. Just realistic."

Georgie put down her fork and raised her eyes. "I know I haven't been much of a wife these last several months. All right, I haven't been a wife at all. I don't blame you for seeing someone else, not a bit. But why do the kids have to know about it? How do you think they'll feel when it's over, when we . . ." She shrugged.

"When we what? What?" Lew said, close to her face.

"Get back together," Georgie said, polishing off the braised celery. She heard only her own chewing, as if through a muted microphone. Then silence. She looked up, then looked up again. He was staring at her.

"That's why you called, isn't it. That's what this is about," Lew finally said.

"I called because I wanted to see you. Because I feel like I've come out of a dense fog. I want to come home, where I belong. I know I'm ready now."

"Ready?" Lew said.

"Yes!" she said eagerly. "I really am, Lew. It'll be a whole new beginning for us. As for . . . Libby . . . I saw someone for a while too. None of that matters. We've got a lifetime binding us, children." She watched Lew struggling to take in what she was saying. She saw the pain in his face and thought of what an enormous relief it must be to have her back, to have their lives back. She loved him then; he was warmth and comfort and safety. How could she find this again, where would she start?

"Georgie, I want a divorce."

She dropped her eyes. It felt like her body was falling.

"I'm sorry," Lew said. "Truly sorry."

She was motionless except for her brows, arching of their own will, trying to hold her face together.

"When you said you wanted to see me, I thought that was what you wanted to talk about. I'd just been about to call *you.* Georgie, all these months we haven't laid eyes on each other, we've talked on the phone like, I don't know, ex-roommates who didn't have anything in common any more except . . . knowing too much about each other."

"And children," she said, dragging it up from somewhere.

"Yes. Children. Who are living their own lives now. In the beginning, I was devastated. I won't deny it. Every day I'd go to work and come home like a mindless robot. What the hell would I do without you? The house became impersonal, or maybe I was looking at it for the first time; you always filled it up so. Once I walked in the door and for a second or two I thought I was in the wrong place, I didn't recognize my own home.

"All I wanted was for you to come back, that's all I thought about. Your absence was the problem, your presence the solution. But when you're alone a lot, and you're not used to it, a curious thing happens. You go from self-pity and obsession to thoughts of survival, and from there, rationality starts creeping in. Had I been happy? Had either of us been happy? I loved you, but it was an uphill battle from the start, and I never got there, Georgie. We both know that. And then I thought, what's 'happy'? We're not kids, we're supposed to know better than to imagine we can beat reality.

"Then I met Libby. It was awkward at first, two people dying on the vine, shoved together by well-meaning friends. We went to a dinner party, both of us under duress, imagining the other was up for it. We had a hell of a time trying to feign interest, trying to remember how to *do* that. Finally I took her home, and when we got to her door I was so relieved I guess I muttered something about a lovely evening. That's when it happened, she looked at me and suddenly she just started to laugh. She tried to hold it in but it was impossible . . . and then I was laughing, I laughed so hard I had tears in my eyes. We admitted we'd had a perfectly horrible time and then somehow we got to talking, right there on the front step. We were like a couple of kids, telling each other everything. Then we went in and made bacon and eggs, opened a bottle of champagne, and watched an old movie until 3:00 A.M. We've been together ever since."

"So now you know what 'happy' is," Georgie said. "It's not knowing, not believing what will happen later, the warts that will grow, the sores that will fester, the juice that will dry up on you. You want to prolong it, and for that you'll grow old with a stranger!"

"Georgie. We're the strangers."

"What happened to that rational thought that was creeping in? We've been together most of our adult lives, we have three children, a history. You haven't shared anything with her except puppy love, a little gray around the edges." Her head was pounding but her tongue rattled on, a curling, disconnected thing. "I thought male gonads reached their high point at eighteen. Are you defying science?"

His chin was resting in his hand while he took this, blinking. He looked like a child with a secret that if you beat him he still wouldn't spill. She hated him for it.

"Do you love me?" Lew said.

Her mouth dried up.

"I said, do you love me. Do you? Do you?"

The cab ride home was swift. Georgie stared through the window and mostly saw herself. Mercifully, her brain slept.

twenty-three

It was mid-October and felt like August. Terrence and Beth were sharing a bench by the river with a woman who had the Sunday *Times* and a Pekingese on her lap, and an umbrella overhead that she had fastened to the back of her seat. The umbrella wobbled and fell; the woman put her dog down, put the fat pile of papers down and refastened the umbrella, then hauled the *Times* back onto her lap, along with the Pekingese. When the umbrella fell again, as they knew it would, their offer to help was airily dismissed. Terrence and Beth stole looks at each other, barely able to contain their laughter, as the umbrella wobbled and fell again and again, and the Pekingese and the *Times* went down and up, down and up. Each time the woman repeated her actions exactly, without a hint of impatience, as if this ritual of preparation followed a sorcerer's formula for angelhood.

Beth's own preparations that morning had been mindless

and predictable until she came out of the shower and noticed that her hair needed a touch-up; in fact, her roots were very much in view. This took her by surprise; she was normally fastidious about her hair, having it colored even before the need became apparent. Now here she was on a Sunday, stuck with her sudden awareness. And curious, too. She pulled her hair back and examined the roots: they weren't exactly white or brown or reddish but a combination of all these that was momentarily mesmerizing. She tried to imagine a full head of hair of this mixture and couldn't; it would take forever for it to grow out, and matching the combination was impossible. She supposed she could cut it all off, that would speed things up, but she'd as likely cut off an arm. Still, she attempted to fabricate various short styles with pins and combs. How had she not noticed this new growth before? She couldn't tear her eyes away, wondering who was under there.

That was when he asked her; walked right in and said, just like that, "What would you think about getting married?"

"To whom?" she had said, ever quick on her feet, and closed the door on his only slightly amused face, explaining she had to pee. What flashed through her mind was a vision of Keifer Sutherland, Donald's pubescent boy, who had just recently played a twelve-year-old and was now married to a woman of forty. Did *her* roots show? How did it feel, waking up next to a face that showed no signs of living? Terrence had a face that would resemble a road map soon enough, scattered routes were already visible. Was that it, then—the esthetic quality of their pairing, the need not to jolt the audience as they played out their lives? She got herself dressed knowing full well what she wanted, trying to assess the degree of foolishness it would take.

Terrence told himself he would ask her again, when she had

quit agonizing over growing old before his time. For now, they were on the promenade in Brooklyn Heights, watching the offering of the umbrella and trying not to laugh.

A few days later, on a morning that was, they thought, fittingly gray and chill after a week of summerlike sunshine, Dale met Suzanne at a coffee shop on the West Side, away from the agency. His smile was crooked. "One of October's little jokes," he said, by way of a greeting.

"Are we in trouble?" she ventured, unable to hold back, wanting him to spill what he knew from his sources, which was probably nothing. But then, seeing his eyebrows arch in mock disbelief, she tried another tack. "Exactly how much trouble are we in?"

Dale sighed. "We've been struck by a six-foot pole. Given the lack of subtlety such an instrument presents, it's been suggested we might have had the sense to duck."

The pole was, she knew, Justine Mitchell, who was actually six foot three and had suffered a tortured adolescence attempting to hunch herself into an acceptable size. Now this senior female executive from the merging company wore stiletto-thin high heels and red dresses and a horribly expensive ankle-length fox coat, the better to shamelessly thumb her nose at short people. This included Suzanne, one of two ranking females at Damon & Moore; the other, a brilliant research and development vice president, was immersed in stats and disinterested in power, thus posing no threat. Suzanne, on the other hand, was perceived by Justine to be in Justine's way.

Suzanne felt as if she'd been done in before the battle was joined, but in truth she had taken Justine's measure almost instantly. At a get-acquainted cocktail party for top management of the two firms that were becoming one, where everyone smiled confidently and exuded a cooperative spirit while secretly measuring their chances for survival and plotting how to improve the odds, Suzanne saw this surprisingly young, rather startling apparition across the room and knew its claws were drawn.

Then how had she let things come to such an abysmal pass, not quite over and done with, but dangerously close? It wasn't her personal life, she'd learned long ago the necessity of separation and in fact could, like many others, immerse herself in work quite successfully when all else was failing. Nor was it her penchant for self-doubt, her tendency at times of stress to feel the fraud she always secretly suspected she was; not this time. After years in the fray, Suzanne knew that the race didn't always go to the swift and sure, or even the best and brightest. No, it was the gamesman, the player who stayed the course, quivering with vigilance. Justine fed on contention, it kept her adrenaline pumping, her every maneuver oiled with significance; she was a natural. Suzanne was a reluctant student, but a good one. It occurred to her now that at precisely the moment when her own senses should have been atingle, she was disengaged. That is to say, not attentive to this palace rumble. But it was work, nonetheless, that held her in thrall; she had begun the transition from desire to daring, and was gathering herself up for a different life. The working life of a painter. That she had made this internal journey she found astonishing; it seemed to have leapt out at her like a surprise gift, when in fact she'd been trekking through the miasma of her own misgivings and apprehensions for years, gathering steam, preparing to breast the tape.

The problem was, what she did affected others, most notably Dale. For as she went, her group went; as her star rose or fell, so did theirs. In this climate, her "downfall," which is how it would be perceived, would make it difficult, if not impossible, for many of her people to hang on. And so she felt at once the extraordinary freedom that comes with the decision to step away and into one's own sphere, and the weight of unfinished business in a world of other people.

Dale told Suzanne what he'd been able to piece together about Justine's foray into their territory, becoming more animated as he saw indignation spread across her face, which was, he realized, precisely the reaction he hoped to elicit. He had planned to tell her she was not responsible for him, to urge her to fly away to her destiny and leave this mongrel world behind, but he couldn't get the words out; this was his life! He was counting on her and she knew it, just as she knew it wasn't his life, he was extremely talented and could get numerous other jobs. He was panicking, that was all. She thought it allowable; he thought it reprehensible, and prayed for the return of his better self.

Still, it was Georgie who called them together that weekend. It wasn't Lew and his Libby that rankled; she had even gotten over her bout of self-loathing for having flung herself backward in time at the first sign of disappointment in the present, acting the part of the predictable, professional ex-wife. What prompted her was a strong desire to cook for her friends, as opposed to selling her culinary treasures to strangers, and to share conversation with these particular women, to whom she had nothing, or almost nothing to prove. Also, she was convinced she was on the menopausal edge and would be overboard momentarily: she wanted company.

It was Saturday. The day had been brutal, Georgie having to put the finishing touches on two different dinners she'd prepared the day before and deliver them to opposite ends of Manhattan just as the area was being whipped into a wet and windy frenzy by a hurricane called Flora that flew nearby. She came home soaked and bedraggled, about as eager for company as a prom queen with chicken pox. But as soon as she began getting the food, the apartment and herself together, an old feeling of anticipation came over her that she recognized as indigenous to Saturday night. It was Georgie's contention and, she was sure, Sandra Dee's, that Saturday was the one night with a distinctly penetrating power.

They arrived within moments of each other, made anxious by her summons and the possibility that, while several months had passed since her suicide attempt, perhaps they had diverted their attention too soon. But the Georgie before them in her newly favorite Day-Glo shirt was neither jittery nor apprehensive; *what,* then? They couldn't guess.

Soon it didn't matter. They drank wine, just enough to slow their consumption of Georgie's spinach phyllo pastries, which she'd cadged from one of her dinner deliveries, to a less-conspicuous gastronomical frenzy.

"I hope you got paid fairly for these," Suzanne said, resting.

"What's fair?" Georgie asked.

"Oh, I'd say an amount so high that if one had to ask, one couldn't afford it."

"Too low," Beth said.

"Hah!" Georgie snorted happily. "I don't suppose I could convince you two to put your money where your mouths are, so to speak. Could I?" This last was said as a sudden afterthought, surprising all of them, including Georgie.

"What do you have in mind?" Beth said, excited at this turn of events.

"I don't know, it just . . . popped out."

"Georgie," she pressed. "Where did it pop *from?*"

"Well, have you ever gone to Jean Pierre's, in the Eighties? It's just a small place, a hole in the wall really, but the smells that emanate from it are rapturous. They're Belgian, Jean and his wife, and they do catering, gourmet meals to go, that sort of thing. Of course the food's incredible, so they're always busy. Once I discovered it I became a Jean Pierre groupie, I couldn't stay away. But I always found myself wishing I was on the other side of the counter."

"But that's a wonderful idea!" Beth said, Suzanne concurring at once. "You could open a place of your own."

Georgie looked like she could be convinced. "Really? Do you think so?"

This launched a discussion about capital, locations, menus, marketing—Georgie talking about business! And she had thought she couldn't possibly feel so alive. Of course she would never actually do this, how could she? But the illusion of credibility was powerful stuff, and Beth and Suzanne fed it. She fed them stuffed chicken breasts with lemon caper sauce.

Over coffee, she tried to project her menopausal life. "Lew will marry Libby and redecorate my house, probably in Sante Fe peach. I'll become one of those Barbara Pym ladies with a hot plate and the hots for the vicar."

"Barbara Pym ladies don't wear hightop sneakers," Beth said, eyeing Georgie under the table. "Certainly not with Hot Sox."

"Besides," Suzanne said, "where will you find a vicar on the Upper East Side?"

"Go ahead, make light of it, but the awful truth is that we're considered to have peaked. Men the same age are just beginning to be taken seriously . . . God, look in the papers, we *know* some of those people who are running things. We knew them way back when, which would scare the hell out of anyone. So why do they get to play so much longer than we do?"

"Ah, Georgie, you have to keep up with your reading," Beth said. "Haven't you seen that article they run once a year in women's magazines, the one with the shocking headline, 'Over Forty and Still Fabulous!'? Of course, no one questions what fabulous *is*—fabulous is looking like Jane and Linda and Racquel and Cher, all of whom reveal their outermost secrets as you read on." Beth sighed. "We're the same suckers we always were. You could reduce the national debt significantly with what we spend on our hair; you could probably run a small country with the profits from all those breakthrough creams we apply so hopefully, so childishly, to our aging skin, all thought overrun by this tribal belief in potions, in miracles. Such frightened, pathetic creatures we are." Especially herself, she thought.

"Unfair," Georgie said. "We're the victims, not the perpetrators."

"Not entirely," Suzanne said. "We're still the preeners of this species; it's primarily our sex, liberated or not, that hangs earrings on its ears and drapes itself in furs and curls and colors its hair and paints its toes. And what does this say, if not *look at me, look at ME.* Of course eventually someone looks and says, hmm, a bit long in the tooth, that one." As she said this she suddenly imagined herself the older, wizened child, and Justine the pink, fresh baby, fighting over the same sandbox, and knew immediately who would win. Was that true? Could thirteen years less of age and experience augur so heavily in Justine's favor at Damon & Moore? Did she care? Bloody hell, if they were still measuring a woman's value in juice, she damn well did. Yet she was straining to break loose and have done with it.

Later, having explained the underground war at the agency and her concern for Dale and the others should she lose or withdraw, all in the face of this incredible thing, her finally emerged courage to follow her heart's desire and paint, she felt spent. What was she to do? Those magicians, her old friends, promised to answer that, but first, a toast to the artist! Which was the answer.

Beth tiptoed into Terrence's bedroom and sat on the floor next to the bed. She watched him sleep for a time, her chin resting on the mattress. She could see that he was forming while she was still refining; she could see the years ahead of them, years when he'd become who he would be, while she trod water wildly to keep up. Then she saw those same years without him. She got up unsteadily, leaned over his sleeping figure and whispered, "I would say yes," confident he didn't hear, when a hand reached out and grabbed her, pulled her onto the bed on top of him, and held her very tight.

Georgie started to clean up, and stopped. How odd, she thought, the three of them together as always and yet the initiator, Georgie herself, hadn't brought them a problem; in fact, something was very much right. She saw now that the notion of a store she could work from, a place of her own where wondrous offerings could be made and sold, had been in her mind for weeks. She just needed to say it out loud, to try it out on her tongue and the air and on an audience before whom she felt fearless.

What were friends for?

twenty-four

Suzanne had sold one painting during her gallery showing, and Paul Salazar was holding on to a second one that he thought might interest a client who was due back from Europe momentarily. That meant she had actually made eight hundred dollars in her new life: another twelve hundred might or might not be forthcoming. Even on the galvanizing premise that such a fortune would continue on a regular basis, it was clear that once she left Damon & Moore her homesteading sights would best be set on addresses with RFD numbers, not to mention her diet, which had been made rich and controlled by years of nibbling on fancy lunches, as was the corporate way.

"Eat Velveeta," Georgie the gourmet cook advised, "it's soothing, like Spencer Tracy and gravy sandwiches. Remember when Lucky Strike meant fine tobacco, and fifteen-year-old girls were children who didn't say fuck, or do it? That's Velveeta. Put it on a saltine; on a rice cracker it becomes desensitized." Mostly, it stuck in Suzanne's teeth, but it was better than what Frank Damon had to offer.

"It's crazy, what happened," Frank said, like an old friend who had watched a natural disaster with her and could, as a survivor, ruminate on the wonder of it all. "You know it has nothing to do with you, with your abilities, your talent, you *know* that. I just don't want to see you leave because of this, although God knows you'd be worth a bundle to a lot of shops in this town. Cripes, you could start your own shop if you wanted to, no question." And Suzanne said, "Criminy, could I?" Frank looked at her long and hard and decided to shut up. He had just offered to fold her, and her group, under the aegis (thumb) of Justine Mitchell, explaining that while in any merger one side is proved the stronger—which in their case was the other side—he and Bill Damon had insisted, absolutely insisted that Suzanne and her people be protected. "We take care of our own," he said, a crown of thorns on his head, the blush of loyalty on his face.

Of course that was before the wind shifted, as winds so unexpectedly often do. Within three days of this discussion, a conversation between John Hanna and one of his close friends, who happened to be the head of a soft-drink company, changed the balance of power at Suzanne's agency and not so incidentally cast a glow over Suzanne that all but shrouded Justine Mitchell.

She knew nothing of this when Frank and Bill took her to lunch, ostensibly to continue a tradition they'd established over the years and, she figured, to court her back into the fold, as she still had not formally agreed to their proposition. They knew nothing of her desire to leave the corporate world altogether and seriously apply herself to her art, regardless of any machinations at Damon & Moore. And so, equally ignorant, they each heard what they thought they knew, until it finally dawned on them that the scenario had changed.

"Let's get down to cases," Bill Moore said, in his direct, fatherly style. "We want you to stay; we *need* you to stay. You're the best we have. And we're damn well not going to dismantle Damon & Moore because of this merger; we're not going to let anyone roll over our people, that wasn't part of the deal."

"Then how does Justine get to roll over me?" Suzanne asked. "Was that a codicil to your agreement? Should I be flattered to be singled out?" She felt fearless and harmless all at once; nothing to lose, nothing to gain.

Bill shifted in his seat, a signal to Frank to take it from here that Suzanne recognized from their many strategy sessions together.

"Suze," he began, "I did a stupid thing and I apologize profoundly for it. I should never have caved."

It occurred to Suzanne that he was actually caving now, for all his display of guileless regret. But why? What pressure could possibly have been brought to bear, and from whom?

"What Frank is trying to say is that we allowed ourselves to get pushed around because we were new at this; but you don't lose your principles that easily. You're part of our team, you always were, and we mean to keep that team intact." He shifted.

"You're not going to report to Justine Mitchell, or anyone else for that matter, except Bill and me. Period," Frank said. "We took care of it and that's that, everything's just the way it was before; nothing's changed."

She looked at her heroes, her knights at the rescue, and knew that in fact everything *had* changed. But she had to wait until dessert was over, like any good client, before she knew what they were selling. The Delite account; they wanted her to handle the creative on the final pitch—but this had been the other side's prospect, it made absolutely no sense that they'd turn it over to Suzanne or anyone else from the old Damon & Moore, not at this juncture. Her mind racing, she thanked them with controlled enthusiasm and assured them she would consider it; this caused Frank Damon to consider it done, despite what he argued was merely a flash of pride on Suzanne's part. Bill Moore knew better, and thought Suzanne had a bigger offer, which he intended to counter with whatever it took.

Dale should have been delighted at what appeared to be a reprieve; Suzanne should have felt more sanguine about leaving in these circumstances, her group intact, as opposed to the appearance of having been forced out and the reality of her coworkers' jeopardy. But when one wins without yet having seriously engaged the enemy, the whimper of victory is overshadowed by a gnawing *why.* As Bill Moore began the arduous wooing he believed "creatives" couldn't resist, Suzanne began to realize that for some reason she and Dale were not only wanted but absolutely essential. Culling every possible source, they learned nothing. Justine Mitchell was subdued, even, at times, obsequious; everyone else was blank.

The day before Suzanne had agreed to give Bill Moore her answer, John Hanna called. It seemed he had been in Japan and hadn't the chance to ask if his recommendation to old Ed Harte at Delite had panned out; did she owe him one, or didn't she? So that was it. Knowing nothing about the political maneuverings within the agency, only that it was merging with one of the contending agencies for Edwin Harte's considerable business, John Hanna had innocently and fervently suggested to Harte that he now had the opportunity to test the mettle of the best creative team in the business. Harte, in turn, had his people specifically request Suzanne and Dale.

Ahh, in like Flynn. But of course Suzanne knew that if the agency didn't get the Delite account, all best would be off; that is to say, all promises. The next morning she was in Bill Moore's office promptly at nine to decline coffee and come to the point. Frank Damon was all smiles.

"Here's the deal: I'm leaving Damon & Moore—wait, wait, I'm not going to another agency, I'm going to paint. You know, with a brush, on a canvas?"

"Suzanne, for God's sake, do you have any idea what we're dealing with here?" Frank blurted.

"As a matter of fact, I think I do." She looked from one to the other. "I have a proposal, if you're willing to listen."

Frank looked at Bill, who nodded.

"I'll stay long enough to work on the presentation for Delite, with the understanding that Dale is taking over as senior vice president and creative director. His appointment will be officially made and released to the press before we make our pitch to Delite. If we get the business, I'll agree to continue on a consulting basis if the account requests it." It seemed to Suzanne a safe enough supposition that if they did not get the account, Dale's status would remain the same for at least a number of months, with agency morale at a low ebb and the need for an appearance of stability. By then he'd have this new title under his belt to trade on should he have to; Suzanne believed he'd prove to be remarkably adept, serving Damon &

Moore so well that any residue of bitterness would disappear in direct proportion to the billings his work attracted and kept. Bill Moore wanted the Delite account, all ten million dollars' worth, and would, she was certain, offer his wife up for exotic favors if he thought it would help. As it was, he merely had to say yes to Suzanne, and he did.

They had two weeks, having pissed away the third, as Frank Damon put it, trying to get their team in place. The work done by the original creative group, the one that had gotten the agency into the finals on Delite, was passed on to Suzanne's team with barely concealed rage. Suzanne liked what she saw, and was about to ask those responsible to stay on the project and work along with her when Dale suggested another tack: "Tell them we *need* them, just say it outright; God knows it's true." She told him to do it himself, and it was the last official thing she would tell him. He was, after all, in charge: the *New York Times* and *Ad Week* said so. She loved watching him measure up.

She herself was winding down; it was most peculiar, as if some new strain had penetrated her system and altered its basic mechanism, loosening the springs. She was not lethargic exactly, but expansive; she couldn't seem to tunnel into the work at hand as she always had in the past. She cared less, of course. Having made the decision to leave this world and its particular peculiarities for one of her own making, she was like a woman in the throes of divorce who is still, unaccountably, living with her husband, jerking her head to clear it, trying to remember why she wasn't gone. Grace notes needed to be struck, a bargain kept, before the moment could be seized. And finally, after two weeks of arduous work, tortuous misgivings and low humor, which bound the new group under Dale's tutelege into a familial gang of paranoid schizophrenics, all of whom remembered to wear shoes to the Delite presentation, it was over. Ed Harte congratulated them personally on a job well done, even though they didn't get the account. But who would have thought that Lucite, the new teen queen of the mall—who was to star in their proposed extravaganza—could be undone by Minnie Mouse as Delite's spokesperson? Ed's people explained as how an animated character like Minnie couldn't possibly destroy their image by getting herpes, blowing dope, becoming a lesbian or shaving her head, which was more than you could promise with Lucite, and of course they understood. Dale's star was at its zenith despite the loss, primarily because he had successfully melded a group from the old Damon & Moore with one from the merging agency and, in effect, created the prototype that the partners of the new shop hoped to achieve. Suzanne was free to go, and she went.

It took some getting used to. She awoke each morning, from habit, in time to get to the office, but instead of making herself up, drawing from a limited range of acceptable themes, she cleaned her face, brushed her hair and tugged on anything comfortable and handy. It was an odd feeling walking east for the papers, when nearly everyone else was hurrying westward to work: Sunday for Suzanne, Monday for the rest of the world? But then, after scanning the endless stream of violence and despair that was called news, she settled down to work of her own. Her apartment was not the place to do this, not on a full-time basis, and she knew it. Still, she felt an exhilaration she couldn't yet place—was it like playing hooky? Like being set free from the real world? But it couldn't be, she had a family to support. It was something else, then, a state that would reveal itself in time. She decided to wallow in it and see what developed.

Daniel and Annie knew she was working at home now, of course, yet each day they found her there they seemed surprised. Watching them go about their silent business once they clambered through the door, suddenly witness to their particular patterns of reentry to home base, she was momentarily stunned by her ignorance of this part of their lives. She knew it was futile to regret the road not taken, and irrational to imagine she did on such flimsy evidence. The fact was that she had blossomed and excelled at Damon & Moore for twenty years, if such quaint benchmarks applied anymore, and her children seemed to have emerged generally sound of mind and body, even thriving. Now *she* was moving on, something they did perpetually.

There was a world going on in her building that she hadn't been privy to before: domestics wheeling children, hauling laundry and flirting with doormen, mailmen whom she'd never seen, women who stayed home with their toddlers, grade school children barreling through the lobby, a retired couple bundled up sportily for their daily walk, a widow off to the museum or lunch . . . these were people who tended to speak to one another, whereas the office-bound on rush-hour elevators tended to stare at the floor indicator, impatient for L. Suzanne's workdays now didn't have an exact pattern, and so she fell into neither category—it suited her to allow each day to speak for itself.

She began looking for studio space in earnest when the smell of paint in the apartment became overpowering, as did her need for a place to go to that was unqualifiedly her own. Eventually she found what she could afford, a room just below Gramercy Park, available for six months on a shared basis with another artist who worked there at night. One section of the studio had a platformed area that served as an effective separation, and was the other artist's place of choice. Suzanne was thrilled with the rest. The building looked like an old garage, and in fact had a wide wooden door that had to be raised up to be opened. The first few floors were occupied by a company that manufactured household items of the sort that usually bore the label "Made in Taiwan." The third floor housed a spiritual advisor who was rarely there during the day, but sometimes left an odor from her nighttime encounters that defied description or destruction; Suzanne called it "eau de Stephen King." It didn't matter. Nothing mattered but the fourth floor, from the moment she arrived there each day until the moment she left. It became her haven.

She dreamed of Neal occasionally, sometimes fitfully, but mostly she felt a curious floating sensation where once she had felt the active state of love. As far back as she could remember, being without a man had always triggered the assumption that being with a man would make it all right again, "it" being her life. And so she'd never exactly chosen a man so much as gratefully acknowledged any move toward her as proof of her worth. Whoever looked her way, she'd view through eyes colored by childhood dreams and adult fantasy, by quirky litmus tests of unknown origin, painting him over, making him fit. She had thought her life depended on it. Yet here she was, manless, breathing with unremarkable regularity. Gone was the heightened intensity of a love affair that never got beyond its beginnings to the naturalness of a middle place, and with it, the heat of girlish dreams. She felt weightless, graceful, swimming toward herself.

Wishing to cheer her on, friends told her how brave they thought she was to leave a lucrative career and do the thing which mattered most. But she hadn't felt particularly brave, it hadn't seemed to be a question of courage so much as conviction and desire, and the more her break with security was celebrated the less brave she felt. People around her spoke wistfully of their own daydreams, coaching a high school football team, buying an inn in Vermont; then they shrugged, sighed with the specificity of the encumbered grown-up, and returned to whatever office spawned the income and the malaise to which they had become accustomed. For the most part, they were glad someone had done it; someone else, not them.

Within a matter of weeks she felt as if she'd shed every last vestige of her other life, just dropped its pieces like layers of insulation until the air suddenly hit her skin and tingled. She had turned inward, as if, having finally wrung form dry, she could now deal with substance. Things popped into her head like so many jack-in-the-boxes set free. It was astounding, the stashing she had done all those years on the run, the sweeping, the tidying. She had taken no time for reflection, had kept the way clear and told herself this was good, she had a job to do and a family to keep. It seemed to her now that Neal had been the perfect fit for that galloping life, imagining a destination yet never having to deal with its fruition. With Neal she hadn't had to be careful what she wished for; she knew it wouldn't come true.

Dale kept in touch, calling every morning because their patter at the beginning of the day had as much to do with pumping his adrenaline as several cups of coffee. Gradually he tapered off, and settled into calling her a few times a week. He missed her terribly.

"Is this like divorce?" he asked. "I feel like I'm walking around with one shoe on and one shoe off; everything is lopsided, but only to me." Even under deadline his calls were more liable to be funny than frantic. This was, after all, just a business; it could be left. But Dale would leave, he often promised, with a dramatic flourish; he'd be the Gable character from the film classic *The Hucksters,* finally dredging up the decency to tell off Sidney Greenstreet's embodiment of the quintessential client, a wheezing, spitting, fat and conscienceless worm. Dale conjured Sidney up often.

On this particular morning, the day after a light snow that was quickly turning to ice, Suzanne was home with the flu and had not seen the papers when Dale called to read her an item about Beth and *The Morning Show* having parted company. Surprised at this news, she suddenly realized that she hardly knew what day of the week it was anymore, much less what was actually happening. When had she last talked with Beth?

She dialed her at once and poured out her guilt and concern to a machine, which made her feel much better; then worse. It was too easy.

twenty-five

"She hasn't been out in a week," Georgie said, nodding toward a barely recognizable Beth stretched comfortably on the couch, reading. "She sees no one, talks to no one, and has done everything in her power to look like someone else—who, I don't know; just someone else. Other than that, everything's perfectly normal."

"She exaggerates, as always," Beth said, without looking up. "I see her, I talk to my editor, and I am not trying to look like someone else. It's my own self she's not used to, that's all."

Suzanne crossed to the couch in her coat and boots and sat on the edge, to peer at Beth's own self.

"You look awful," Beth said, returning her stare.

"Thanks," Suzanne croaked. It was clear she was feverish. They helped her off with her layers of clothing, sat her in a chair with a footstool, wrapped her in an afghan and plied her with tea and honey. All the while she snuck looks at Beth's naked face, and the scraggly, lifeless hair of no discernible color that was left on her head. She looked smaller, even frail, as if her hair had been what had given her strength and stature.

"Did you have to do it quite that way?" Suzanne asked, carefully, as if of a child who had just finished a tantrum. "Couldn't you have had it done professionally, just sat in a chair and asked for a short haircut?"

"I don't know," Beth said, honestly enough. "But I do remember the awful understanding that if I waited, if I didn't go with the urge right then, I would lose what little courage I had. Actually I shouldn't call it courage, it wasn't that solid a thing. It was flimsy, heady, more like hysteria—could that be the root of courage? In any case, it got me through. I was just so tired of it, all this business of trying to hold on to our looks as if we were holding on to our lives."

"But isn't that exactly it?" Georgie said. "Why else would we succumb, forking over hard cash at the mere mention of elasticity, trembling with hope at each new discovery that promises to rid us of this or that dead giveaway."

"Of course we're bombarded with it daily, the fearful persuasion, the soft lies," Beth said, "but I'd begun to perceive a more sinister message. Remember the loonies who insisted that if you played rock music backward the lyrics were transformed into Satanic inducements, causing one to wonder if they ever listened to it frontward, which would have saved them all that bother? Or those eagle-eyed keepers who spied sexual organs afloat in a glass of Scotch in a print ad? Well, the subliminal communiqué I received said that wrinkles were actually fault lines—we were at fault somehow, and we'd better right ourselves or get dragged out to the barn and shot."

"So you decided to dabble in the future, a guinea pig for the rest of us. Well, what have you learned?" Suzanne said.

"No sweeping gestures await; I haven't any high-flown, universal convictions or solutions. Well, is Katharine Hepburn really happier than Zsa Zsa? Is there something noble, even graceful, in accepting whatever nature, and your genes, dish out? If you succumb to vanity, and avail yourself of all the antidotes you can lay your hands on, does that automatically make you shallow and pathetic?"

"No, just better looking," Georgie said.

Suzanne tugged at Beth's blanket. "The fact remains that when a person cuts her hair with what appears to have been a machete, so that what was once shining and pampered is suddenly, forgive me, but *weedy* comes to mind, the change is extreme, even shocking. It could scare a person's friends."

"But age is shocking, isn't it?" Beth said. "And that's all you're looking at. I still bathe, and brush my teeth, and shave my legs. I observe the civilized amenities. I haven't turned into a crone overnight. But I asked myself, how are you going to handle the steady physical deterioration that will only speed up during whatever years you have left? Are you going to continue to flail at it, or are you going to give in, and let yourself meld with this external, other being who's been waiting for you all along, this older woman? And what would become of my interior life if I kept on expending all that energy, all that hope, on preserving the package, as if it, and my value, were one and the same?"

Suzanne hadn't taken her eyes off Beth, who was, despite her rashness, still quite beautiful, although oddly so, with the alarming frailty of a hungry child. "Can you fit this into some kind of sequence for me?" she asked.

"What do you mean?" Beth said.

"I mean, was it before or after Terrence proposed, and you and the network decided to part for a while?"

Beth sat with her legs crossed, a lean, pop-eyed Buddha, and tried to divine a pattern.

It had started, she thought, that day in the shower when she realized she had forgotten to touch up her hair, and was suddenly alert to what was underneath. She couldn't take her eyes off that new possibility, it was almost as if someone else was growing underneath her skin, just waiting to take over, to become her. She was less frightened than curious. Of course she knew she could keep that other under control for the time being; all it would take was the right chemical application carefully timed, and she'd never have to see it again. Still, part of her wanted to set her older self free and let it overtake her. Was that who she was now? Was that the reality, and the picture she chose to present a sham? She had just begun to pursue this thought when Terrence had burst in, talking of marriage. This was, she knew, his way of testing for legitimacy; if she laughed, he would have retreated, his own laughter joining hers, half convinced that he was in on the joke. Instead she had been flippant, coy, hoping to hold him in abeyance while she considered metamorphosis. Would he even want her, stripped of her veneer? It mattered terribly. She wanted him to want her. Yet she felt driven to peel away her façade; impatient, even, to see underneath.

When she did it, when she chopped at her hair, Terrence was at first astounded, then aggrieved. It seemed to him an irrational act precipitated by his proposal, a child's stamping demand for real proof of love. But if it was a test at all, it was of her own self, this new self. No longer focusing on the difference in their ages, she was trying to adjust her inner eye, learning to make concessions, allowances, preparing for change. She tried to tell him it had nothing to do with him, with them. That the provocation was entirely personal. But he seemed to believe that when a woman was in love, neither her actions nor her motives were ever entirely personal. She could have admitted he had a point, but she didn't.

She couldn't remember the day that she had cut her hair in any particular detail. It could have been any day, with its random incidents and accidents. It wasn't as if she had awakened with some grand design, however flawed; she had even slept well. She did recall flashing scissors, and hearing the crunch as each clump of hair was cut through.

"I still love you," Terrence had said when he saw her.

"What do you mean 'still,' " Beth said, "are you informing me that you're big enough to overcome this terrible obstacle . . . this gray matter? That despite looking older, I'm still lovable?" Oh, how righteous she was, how primed for battle—how insistent on finding an enemy.

"This isn't something that happened, that befell you," Terrence said angrily. "You chose to do it precisely because you wanted to know what my reaction would be, you needed to know. As if how you look is what binds me to you, keeps me—as if it had everything to do with us!"

"But it's had to do with *me* all of my life," Beth said. "I've been thought of as beautiful, told it countless times by wide-eyed boys and nervous men. I've been treated with the special deference reserved for those among us who emit that shimmering aura, that gossamer glow, and I've accepted it as my due, without reflecting on it. How can you say that how I look has had little to do with us, with your attraction to me or even your attitude toward me, your *idea* of me. Just as now you look at me and you see someone else, someone I'm becoming, and this changes your perception."

He was looking at her, studying her. "Yes. Yes, it does." She waited. "I'm not sure I know you. I'm not sure I know who you are."

Ahh well yes of course, precisely what she thought he'd say, precisely! She stormed out on a wave of probity that ebbed the moment the cold air hit her.

There was no time for second thoughts; she was already late for a meeting at the network. Her agent had said they were close to coming to terms on her new contract, and suggested that a personal visit with the network's chief negotiator would most likely finalize the deal. She didn't want to let it go; now that she had gotten the hang of it, she discovered she rather liked being on the air. Even Terrence said she had improved, so that now the audience could concentrate on her words rather than be distracted by her anxiety.

Terrence. The moment she thought of him, her hand went to her close-cropped hair. It was still there, all right. She had actually done it. And it looked fine. Didn't it look fine?

She went straight to Harvey Davis's office. He was the only person of authority at the network whom she trusted or even understood. Harvey, a pear-shaped man with a drooping mustache, who still couldn't wipe the sandbox grin off his face at having made a success of himself out of Evanderchild High School and City College, looked confused.

"Is that you?" he said.

"It's me," Beth said, innocent, assured.

"I don't believe you," he said, shaking his head as if to clear it of this apparition.

"Is it that bad?" she asked, not really undone, maintaining rather than reverting to type.

"Beth, for God's sakes." He winced at her spiky, jagged hair;

she looked as if she'd been violated. He brought his voice down to its kindly uncle octave. "What, you wanted to be Peter Pan?"

"Do I look like Peter Pan?" she said, settling herself into the couch across from his desk, her coat gathered around her like conviction, her glasses secure, her legs primly together.

"You look like Alice B. Toklas. With a nose job." Harvey got up and joined her on the couch. "Are you all right? Of course you're not all right, how could you do this to yourself if you weren't . . . you *did* do this to yourself? I mean, no one did this to you, did they?"

"Harvey, I didn't steal, maim or kill, I didn't even miss a deadline. I cut my hair. This is a haircut." *(I can handle this.)*

"Beth . . ."

"AND I'm letting my natural color grow in, so it looks a little weird right now, I know, I know. But it's still just a haircut, this is still just hair we're talking about."

"This is television we're talking about," Harvey said.

Beth's eyes flashed. "You mean if I look my age I'm not acceptable? I thought this was a news show, not *Dynasty.*"

"Unfair, and you know it. What you are is a featured player on a pseudo-news program that may differ from all the other pseudo-news programs by virtue of the color of the couch or where they put the goddamn flowers, but we like to tell ourselves it has a certain approach, a certain style. You were chosen to join it because you fit."

"You mean because of the way I look."

"I mean all of it, everything, the way you look and the way you express yourself and the subjects you choose and the kind of people you reach—you're a package, Beth. Everyone on television is a package."

"And the package is devalued now that I have short, graying hair, is that correct?"

Harvey put his hands on her shoulders and squeezed gently. "Beth, I don't see short, graying hair, I see a mess! I see the remains of a beautiful head of hair that's been chopped at mercilessly; I see someone out of control." When she didn't respond he let her go, then stood up. "My advice is, go home and stay home for three or four weeks . . . take a vacation, a leave, whatever you want to call it. Just don't come back until you feel better and you have what could reasonably be called short hair, graying or otherwise. Then we'll see."

Harvey made all the arrangements, covered for her with the producer and covered for the network by advising the lawyers to hold off. The press got wind of the delay and projected the rest.

"So now you're on hold, growing your hair like a good girl while you hide from the world," Suzanne said. "What was the point?"

"Oh, it's not that bad. I go out. I wear hats. It's fun, actually, like playing dress-up. Put on a hat and you become someone else, regal, mysterious, romantic, young . . ."

"How old is Terrence?" Suzanne asked. "I never really knew."

"He's thirty-two and you think that's why I did it."

"Is it?"

Beth was suddenly up and pacing. "All I know is I felt compelled, I had this great desire to strip away all the artful delusion, the sparkle designed to mask what we think of as our imperfections, see what was really there, and accept it without fear; *that* was the point. As if such modern voodoo would unearth a great truth, instead of more questions." She sat down. "My little gesture changed nothing. Even the women's movement hasn't been able to loosen beauty's hold on all of us. We are still defined on some basic level by how we look; even limited by it. Why else would plastic surgery be such a thriving business? And look at us, telling ourselves that liposuction or an eye tuck is the new way for women to take control of their lives! How desperately we try to make it acceptable for enlightened women to remain in the Dark Ages; how frightened we are that our place in the world will disappear, our value disintegrate, if we don't keep our looks up to some ethereal standard. Well, even surgery has its limits. There is an old face waiting for every one of us, even Cher. Maybe I just tried to hurry it up a little, to see if I could manage without the looks I've relied on all my life. If I can stand it, if I don't cave in, will I have become a better person? Can one be genuine, and made up, all at once? Am I beginning to sound like the blind grandfather of *Kung Fu*"?

"What's wrong with a little delusion in a terrifying world?" Georgie asked. "You make it sound as if you were a charlatan, trying to palm off worthless goods with some lowdown razzle-dazzle. This is theater! Life is theater! People have been painting themselves, adorning themselves with one thing or another since the beginning of time, acting at this, playing at that. Even at our most acquisitive or desperate, aren't we still observing tribal custom that has been handed down through the ages? Isn't that part of civilization?

They were discussing the merits of putting the entire Westmore family, cosmetologists to the stars of Hollywood for generations, out of business ("such nice boys," Georgie argued) when Terrence called Beth.

He said, "It feels very peculiar, your being away from me."

He said, "I suppose you *are* beautiful. I admit I've noticed. I've noticed how your mind works and how your hips move, and the way you wet your upper lip when you're struggling for a word or a phrase; must I examine the source of my love and parse it like a sentence? I don't think you mean that. I think something else entirely. Some private rite is going on in that woman's head of yours." And while she had insisted all along this was so, only now was she certain.

"Will you marry me?" she heard him say.

"When my hair is longer than yours."

twenty-six

Georgie had taken more catering orders for the holidays than she could reasonably handle, because she had great difficulty saying no; she feared each client might be her last, each dinner her culinary swan song. When Jack David called to tell her he had inadvertently stumbled upon the perfect location for her food store, she reacted with great agitation. She was too busy; she had too much on her plate already; she couldn't think; couldn't it wait? The truth was, Georgie had gotten herself up for wanting the store, not for having it.

"If you saw this place, you'd know," Jack said. "It has the perfect layout. The front room is just large enough to display a good assortment of take-out dishes—not too few, not too many—and it won't look cramped if a couple of people are there at one time, it'll just look user-friendly. The back room has all the equipment you'll need for your catering service, you won't have to buy a thing. Not one thing."

"It sounds like a kitchen," Georgie said.

"Okay, a kitchen," Jack said.

"So, was it a restaurant or a caterer that failed there?"

"Georgie, no matter where you go someone will have failed there, or had to leave because the rent was too high or they got robbed too often or it was time to move to Florida. You want virgin territory, go to Nome. Otherwise take a look at Ninety-third Street. Georgie, you will fall in love, I promise."

She did. With the block, which was lined with brownstones and some very nearly healthy trees. With the shop's corner location, which seemed highly favorable. Mostly, with the shop itself. Bare as it was, the moment Georgie stepped in she knew she had entered her own magic garden; she was bewitched, enthralled, sold. Then came the matter of money.

"Do you realize these *rents*? And what they want in ad*vance*? I can't let friends put money into this; my God, what if I fail? People fail all the time you know, people much better and smarter than I am, people with ex*per*ience, not ex-housewives who cook!"

"Georgie," Jack said. "I really care for you very much; I liked you the minute we met and I kept liking you even when you got thin, and sometimes I've even fantasized about running off with you despite the fact that my wife would kill me, but you know something, Georgie? One thing I don't fool around with is money."

As her largest investor, Jack took her in hand. First he instructed her on the requirements of a business plan, then helped her write it. Next he dragged her to Long Island City to meet with the de Flavio brothers, three huge Italians with gentle voices who screamed only on the telephone, as when ordering the display cases and counters for Georgie's shop at the best possible prices. In lieu of the cash she did not have, Suzanne offered two of her paintings to warm the walls, and the design for the logo. Beth handed over twenty-five thousand dollars, explaining to Georgie's gaping mouth that as she had made it in television she considered it surreal and would not miss it. Terrence went in for five thousand; Dale sprang for ten. Everything was moving so quickly Georgie felt breathless. Jack hurried her along whenever she showed any signs of flagging, which helped rather than hindered; he seemed to know his customer, because Georgie was gaining confidence by the hour.

Announcement cards designed by Suzanne were sent to every customer Georgie had ever had, every friend of every customer whose name she could remember, and every friend and acquaintance and business associate of each of the investors. Then they concentrated on the neighborhood, sending an announcement to every resident in the shop's zip code.

They couldn't open officially until January; there simply wasn't enough time to make it for the holiday rush. Still, Georgie was stuck with all the orders she had taken on her own, and the need to be at the shop to supervise its design—both at the same time. The problem was solved when Jack suggested she inaugurate her shop's kitchen a little early; she was already paying for the place, there was no law that stated she couldn't use it before they opened officially. It wasn't ideal, what with all the noise and distractions as workmen hammered away, but you'd never guess this watching Georgie as she bounded back and forth, her cheeks flushed with excitement.

When Shawn and Melissa were set loose from their respective schools for Christmas vacation, and Georgie let them in on her venture, they were astonished. Where had this entrepreneurial bent come from, the audacity, the confidence? They were proud of their mother, this new person who had changed dramatically when they weren't looking yet was still recognizable, still familiar. Hanging around Georgie's store those first few days, in between shopping for clothes and presents, they dropped little pellets of news about their father as casually and offhandedly as they could manage, testing what she knew, probing her feelings, wondering about the future in the way children do who travel between their separated parents. And so she learned that Lew was seriously considering marriage to Libby once the divorce was final; that Libby's son was a sophomore in college and, according to Melissa, pretty cute but a dumb-jock type; that Libby's house was up for sale but Lew's (and Georgie's) wasn't. "She's very nice," Shawn said, adding quickly "but she can't cook to save herself." And Georgie thought, Is that what I'm doing, cooking to save myself? It didn't matter; it was working.

In the midst of this hubbub Georgie was given an assignment out of Dickens; two weeks notice that Beth and Terrence were getting married. Quietly, very privately, on New Year's Day, thereafter to celebrate with a small crowd of, say, a hundred, who would be fed unconscionably well by Georgina Brand, of that most coveted catering establishment on the Upper East Side, Entrée Nous.

"Don't trust me with it," Georgie pleaded, "not your wedding, are you mad?" She tried logic. "I'm up to my ears in orders!" Even melodrama. "Small dinners make me crazy, how can you expect me to hold up for a major event, especially with all those news hotshots and actors and God knows who-all you're having?"

"Reporters will eat anything," Beth said.

"Actors don't eat at all, unless they're out of work," Terrence said.

"Then you don't need me!" Georgie tried, failing fast.

"Oh, all right," she said finally. "Sure. Why not?" And got a full hug from Beth that surprised them both; for years they'd been pressing each other's arms, leaning toward each other's cheeks, kissing the air. It had nothing to do with affection or the lack of it, it was what one did; what grown-ups did; what girls did when they became grown-ups.

"There is so much we do without taking notice," Suzanne had said. "I find that I'm noticing everything now, most of all myself. I never took the time; told myself I didn't have the time, that I was just too busy, too pressed. After all, single parent, career woman—who could blame me? Georgie, it frightens me to think that I might never have stopped to notice." Georgie hadn't really understood what Suzanne meant, or perhaps her reflexes took over when she heard such phrases as single parent and career woman: how could a mere housewife, houseperson or whatever epithet they were enamored of this week for the married woman who stays home with her kids possibly know how it feels to be on a treadmill with blinders on, to be so caught up in getting it all done she can't be troubled with which part matters?

Still, here was Georgie trying to remember how she had once become spiritless, not so much an unbeliever as a disbeliever, a spoiler. That was how she saw her old self, for she was conscious now of a new self emerging, a self more like her inner version of Georgie Brand . . . some slim embodiment of her hopes perhaps, her dreams? All those years she had watched herself as one would watch a boring play by a friend—feigning interest, trying to care. She was still very close to that Georgie, she was only a heartbeat away and she knew it. Change was really a matter of moving an inch to this side or that; it could make all the difference, but it was an easy step back.

Beth, who had taken to dropping by the shop to "check on her investment" was like a schoolgirl on vacation, giddy, apple-cheeked, brimming with delight. Her hair had grown in just enough to soften it so that she no longer looked crazed, but rather childish, nearly lustrous. As Christmas drew nearer, though, Beth virtually disappeared, having to prepare all at once for the holidays, a wedding and a honeymoon week in the sun, which meant writing articles to cover her absence along with everything else.

Suzanne, too, was working feverishly, preparing a representational selection of her work on the possibility that she might be commissioned as the artist for the newly refurbished lobby of the building in Boston where John Hanna based his company. Her old mentor and dear friend, and now Neal's boss, John had been as supportive as ever when she broke the news of her leap into unemployment and unequivocation. He knew of course that she was no longer seeing Neal; she sensed he approved, but it was not the sort of thing they discussed, and in any event it had nothing to do with their relationship. Reminded of those last days with Neal when she spoke with John, she was amazed at how readily she had believed that she'd never be able to paint with that intensity again; it was as if her passion came purely from her love affair and the raging angst it had put upon her, as if she hadn't her own well to draw upon, her own essence to fire her senses. John was flying in to look at her work, which he had seen and liked through the years but had never experienced in the heightened state of its current incarnation. He would be overwhelmed, and make a recommendation to the building's board that was too impassioned to be ignored.

It was Georgie's plan to throw a party at the shop's opening, now scheduled for January 2 and seeming even closer than it was because of the towering amount of work that needed to get done preceding it. Jack, who was becoming more of a partner than an investor, turned out to have a facility for unearthing the very best food suppliers in the city and environs, for the specialties Georgie planned to feature, and to love all the necessary calculations that went into the buying and the estimated selling. In fact they were a perfect team, Jack with his business head and great interest in, and love for, food, and Georgie's expertise at what Jack could not do, which was cook. Georgie had a wonderful flair, too, for designing and decorating the shop, and had proved adept at working with the contractor to make the most out of a relatively small space. Thus she and Jack complemented and trusted each other—friends of the very best kind. Even Jack's wife approved wholeheartedly, because, May David confided, his excitement about this new venture had snapped him out of the jaws of boredom and revitalized his life. Georgie certainly hadn't been this wound up in years, her days not just passing but whirling by. Yet her senses were heightened; she had a distinct awareness of texture and substance as never before, even felt at times she could bite the air. She wondered, before dropping off to sleep some nights, if this was going to be it, if she was going to wind up "alone"; that is to say, a single woman with work and friends that she loved.

It never kept her awake.

twenty-seven

To no one's surprise, Christmas had turned out bleak and rainy; old MGM movies were the last purveyors of sleigh bells ringalinging and snowfalls you could count on.

Suzanne and the kids had celebrated Hanukkah, but as always left a small stash of presents aside for Christmas. Daniel and Annie had been with their father the Christmas before, along with the woman he lived with and her two sons. They were nice enough, her ex-husband was nice enough, but who were they? Here was a man called Father on one coast, living with someone else's children on another coast. She couldn't remember anymore why she divorced him, nor did she feel the slightest contention regarding the woman, his second live-in since they had parted. Nice, everyone in California was nice. So she surrounded her children with a yammering array of relatives each holiday that she had them, her parents, her brothers with their wives and children, noisy, opinionated, French. That afternoon, having found a grocery in which to buy the inevitable last-minute quart of milk, Suzanne turned in the driving rain to look at the bare trees in the park. Their brittle, spiky branches were softened by the haze, which seemed to have cast a glow around them. Later, when her phone rang, innocently enough, she would remember that moment, her rapt intensity, even the illusion of peace.

Georgie had spent the day before Christmas, and, it seemed, every day of her life before that, preparing puff pastries, tartlet shells, canapés and bread cases with a variety of fillings that would have made Julia Child proud, most especially the Julia Child who occasionally dropped things on the floor of her television kitchen. Christmas Day Georgie spent with her kids, or two of them. Laura was in Seattle, with her boyfriend's family. This was something new, this boyfriend; the fact that Laura was spending Christmas with his family made Georgie squirm, although she wasn't entirely sure why. She didn't mind Laura having a young man in her life; on the contrary. She didn't mind her daughter spending Christmas somewhere else, this one time. What she minded, she finally realized, was being completely in the dark: his family would be in on this thing from the start, while Georgie made do with letters, phone calls, smoke signals. On the other hand, Tom Golden had flown in from New Orleans to spend Christmas with Melissa, rounding out Georgie's table. She liked Tom enormously for his dry wit, his gentle speech and his obvious love of Melissa, although it was jarring to see him against a New York backdrop. Still, maybe they'd settle here after all—Tom was stronger, wilier than one might think at first glance; probably make mincemeat of the natives, and have them loving it. Georgie thought all this while preparing roast leg of lamb, crisp potatoes, string beans and salad exactly as her children had ordered, when it occurred to her that she might become a grandmother sometime soon. She remembered Beth saying that it seemed to her that she'd walked about for years thinking she was twenty-seven, only to awaken, in a flash, in her forties. That she could remember no crash of cymbals jerking her from her cozy sleep, just that suddenly there it was: life's middle, the cool of the evening.

Before the night was over, Georgie was longing for a respite from the heat of grief.

Beth had never taken a man home to Washington for Christmas, not since her married years with Donald. When she made her way to her mother's during the holidays, she assiduously avoided Christmas Day, always arriving a day or two later. It wasn't her brothers and their wives and children she was avoiding; in fact she was never certain why it was so essential on that particular day that she not be confronted by her mother's distance. For her part, her mother seemed unfazed by the pattern; Beth was simply expected to turn up sometime after the twenty-fifth, nor was she ever pressed by claims to filial devotion to arrive sooner. Still, it had made perfect sense to Beth to be climbing into a taxi with Terrence on Christmas morning and slogging to the airport with a shopping bag of presents, there to take the shuttle to her mother's. Mrs. Taitlow was not especially well and hadn't yet said if she was coming to the wedding, although she had made the observation that second marriages were not worth much fuss. Hearing this, Beth had laughed, and was as amazed as her mother at the sound, however rueful. Her decision to take Terrence home was another milestone of sorts, for she was not seeking to elicit parental approval, or trigger mother love; it was Terrence she wanted to educate, by baring her roots—"Yet again," Beth had joked.

Absolutely no one recognized her on the plane, not that she was generally mobbed by fans. But she'd gotten accustomed, in public, to a murmuring sound in her wake. She didn't miss it exactly, it had even caused her some embarrassment; still it was amazing how quickly one could become dependent upon extra attention and service, almost as if one deserved it. She patted her hair and wondered if she hadn't fallen backward altogether, having made a point theatrically only to prove, the moment consequences were sounded, that it had no weight: her hair was colored again, covering the gray.

"But why are you so hard on yourself?" Terrence had asked. "If you lived in a culture where baldness in women was especially coveted, would it reflect a paucity of intellect, a shallowness of character, to shave your head? We're not discussing nuclear disarmament here, just the human desire to look attractive."

Or, as Georgie had put it, "What are you, Sister Mary Agnes? Even Gloria Steinem streaks her hair, and I'm not so sure about Sister Mary Agnes anymore, either."

The shuttle was jam-packed, slow to take off and even slower to land. The snow had turned to sleet by the time they made it to the taxi line, along with nearly everyone else on their flight. Beth was glad she had worn her red coat; it was a beacon against the gray sky. A young man standing near them, wearing a red scarf, nodded his approval. Terrence held her hand as she got into the cab, and let go only for the moment it took to fold himself in beside her.

Within two miles of the house in Bethesda, on a road called Rock Creek Parkway, a young man with a huge Santa decal on the side of his van skidded out of control and crashed into a taxi with full force, killing the driver and one of his passengers. The other passenger suffered a broken collarbone and several broken ribs. The driver of the van, who had been drinking Coors since breakfast, in keeping with the holiday spirit, was unharmed. It was hours before anyone was notified of the death of Elizabeth Emerson; it was Terrence O'Neil, finally conscious and coherent, who called the family in Maryland, and the family of friends in New York. Her people assumed she would be buried down there, but Terrence balked; he wanted to take her home. It was Suzanne who intervened.

"Her dad's there. I think she'd want to be near him," she said gently.

"Of course. I know. It's just . . . if she's in the family plot then she and I won't . . . I wanted us to be together. I feel like I'm losing my mind!" Suzanne heard an anguished sound that could have been ripped from her own heart, the sudden, shocking awareness of the randomness of life. We make our little dramas, she thought, as if they mattered.

Georgie kept praying she'd wake up in a cold sweat, finally rid of her terrible dream, but it persisted, like one's worst childhood fright. Shawn and Melissa, who had returned to Larchmont with Tom Golden, were back early the next morning hovering over Georgie, afraid to let her out of their sight. They would attend the funeral the following day; they'd known Beth all their lives. Lew called and spoke with Georgie for almost an hour, reliving their past, shoring her up, loving her for the last time; he would come to the funeral too. Laura, out of sync because of the three-hour time lag from Washington state, had trouble securing a flight in time to make the service, but she had to be there and was so propelled that nothing could stop her, and nothing did.

Daniel and Annie, younger than Georgie's children, were nearly stupefied; how could Aunt Beth be dead? Suzanne felt no differently. She had spoken with Terrence about the funeral, forcing herself to affect a calm that sounded, to her own ear, almost savage. Then she holed up in her room and tried to give herself permission to let it all go but she couldn't let anything go, she could only hold on tighter and tighter. And then the phone rang. She picked it up expecting someone in this circle of grief, as if all else had ceased, as if nothing and no one existed beyond it. Then what was this?

He had met her, he said, at the Christmas party at Dale's agency . . . no, he wasn't in advertising, he built solar homes in Connecticut . . . well, the thing was he was an old childhood friend of Dale's partner, the art director . . . was something wrong? She had started crying and really couldn't stop. Finally she heard him say "Easy does it," and she responded automatically, trying to obey, as if she was a child again and could, by being good, make all the bad go away. Then she told him everything. Or what passes for everything when your insides are so knotted that any release, any emission whatever, engenders such relief you feel you've shed a thousand-pound porcupine shirt. He was a good listener, unembarrassed by this outpouring of intimacy from a relative stranger. At the end he said, you must have loved her very much, and for just that second it seemed to Suzanne that he knew precisely the meaning of those words. Then he asked if he might take her to dinner the following week, if she was feeling up to it. She said yes just as easily as she might have said no, seeing little difference; who knew what might happen in a week? She didn't bother to write it down and soon wasn't sure their conversation had actually occurred. He was an engineer, though; not the kind likely to forget.

It would be said later that the funeral was not what it should have been, but then, as Georgie pointed out, it should not have been at all. The two contingents, north and south, knew nothing of each other; they placed themselves like opposing families at a wedding. Terrence, in a wheelchair, was flanked by a man nearly as tall as he with faded red hair that was fast turning gray, and two open-faced young women, one a redhead as well, the other a pretty brunette: his father and sisters. Suzanne and Georgie sat hunched with their children, and on their periphery were Dale, a small group of actors and a dancer and her husband who had been friends with Terrence for years. Beyond them sat a visibly shaken Harold Caso, Beth's old editor and friend; next to him, her ex-husband Donald, most graciously, with his wife.

Nearly everyone went to the grave site, where a maddeningly impersonal service was quickly conducted by a minister with a runny nose. Beth's mother, suddenly recognizable to Georgie and Suzanne, who had only met her once, years before, was so frail, so brittle-thin, that when she shook with her grief they thought she might break in half. They tried to reach her but she shrank from everyone, except for a tall, heavy-set woman called Delilah, who held her protectively, as if she were a child. Eventually the crowd thinned until finally, with their families and friends hanging back, Georgie and Suzanne had Beth to themselves.

They stood there, staring at a hole in the ground, failing to comprehend.

"It's so cold," Beth said. "She hates the cold, she'll freeze." She was pursing her lips to stop them from trembling and blinking to stop the tears; nothing worked. Suzanne reached for her hand.

"Do you remember when Annie got that bee sting and was so horribly sick?" As if either of them could have forgotten the moment when Suzanne's daughter hovered so close to death. "Beth made me concentrate on every funny story about her, so I'd be in practice for when she was eighteen and brought a boy home."

Georgie shook her head yes, affirming this life. "And when I tried to, you know, at the hospital, she said Georgie, what were you thinking, who would make the reservations for our lunches, who would dress Lew?" She tried to laugh but her breath came too short; Suzanne patted her back. Each knew they wanted to stay there forever, and they also wanted to run. Terrence was waiting his turn, Georgie and Suzanne felt his presence even before they saw him. They hesitated, unable to let go, knowing they'd never be exactly whole again. But Beth was his too; his after all. They each hugged him as they passed.

It was such a damnably ordinary winter day, steam puffing from people's lips, the sky foreboding. They'd gotten dropped off in Georgetown on a whim, because neither of them could face the plane ride home just yet: Dale had been enlisted to marshal Suzanne's children, and Georgie's were on their own. They walked arm in arm, past pricey storefronts and junk shops indicative of the area's fragmented alignments with teenagers, upscale government toilers, dowagers and the occasional horde of thugs. They were grateful for the disruption of humanity, grateful to walk among people abstracted by their own thoughts, oblivious to their particular sorrow. They stopped in front of a real estate office and gazed at the photos of townhouses and country homes no longer wanted.

"The mistake is to think that anything lasts," Georgie said.

"Have you?" Suzanne asked.

"What?"

"Thought that anything would last, anything at all."

Georgie saw their reflections in the window. "Us, I guess."

On the shuttle flight home, they sat with newspapers in front of them that remained unread, impersonal tragedy having to wait. When they hit an air pocket it occurred to Georgie that their plane might drop out of the sky, or the sky itself might fall. And how she'd rage at that devil of a God! There was nothing at all unusual about wanting to live, except that Georgie hadn't wanted to bother, that day in her kitchen, a million years ago. Now she was a regular creature, gulping her seconds, her moments.

"I thought this was supposed to happen later," Georgie said. "It's too soon to be losing each other, too soon to have reached the beginning of the end."

Suzanne heard the appeal in Georgie's voice, felt the itch in her own fingers. "I think," she said, seizing at affirmation, breathing it in, "it's just the end of the beginning."

ABOUT THE AUTHOR

ANN BERK, a former television executive, is the author of the novel *Fast Forward,* and numerous articles. She and her husband live in Connecticut.